In This House
A Domestic Discipline Collection

By Rebeckah Markham

The "Beautiful" Stories

The Plan

Mia sat at the small kitchen table where she'd spent the afternoon. When she'd gotten home from the doctor, she simply hadn't had the energy to do anything except finish off an entire bag of chocolate chip cookies. After she'd eaten even the crumbs, she trailed her hands along the plaid pattern of the tablecloth.

She had rested her head on her hands and was staring at the empty cookie bag when Chris entered the room.

"Hi sweetheart," Chris greeted her. "What's wrong?"

Mia looked up at him with a forlorn expression on her face. "I had my doctor's appointment today."

Chris became alarmed. He sat in the chair across from his wife. "What is it? What happened?"

Mia dropped her head into her arms and began to cry. Chris jumped up from his chair and rushed to her side. "Mia, baby, what is it? What happened at the doctor's office?"

Mia raised her head and looked at her husband. He was so loving and so concerned. "She said I have to lose forty pounds!" Mia wailed.

Chris froze for a moment, looking confused. Then he began to laugh.

"It's not funny!" Mia snapped.

"I'm sorry, honey," said her husband, attempting to shape his mouth into a more serious expression. "You looked so sad that I thought you were about to tell me something terrible."

"It is terrible," Mia insisted.

"Honey, it's okay," Chris told her. He wrapped his arms around her shoulders. "What did the doctor say exactly?"

Mia sniffed. "She said that my weight was putting me at risk for Diabetes, high blood pressure and other problems. She also said that it might have something to do with why we're not getting pregnant."

Chris stroked Mia's soft curls. "That must have been hard for you to hear."

Mia nodded. She looked so sad that Chris ached with the desire to make her feel better.

"If the doctor says you need to lose weight, then we just have to follow a plan," said Chris. "That's all. It's not a big deal."

Mia sighed. "You don't understand. I can't do this. My immediate reaction to the news was to eat a bag of cookies. I'm hopeless, Chris!"

"You're not hopeless. You just need some self-discipline," Chris said.

Mia shook her head sadly. "I don't have any."

"Don't be silly," her husband said. He stood up and clapped his hands together. "You can do this."

Mia looked up at him for a long time. "I need you to help me," she finally said.

"Of course I'll help you. We can cook healthy recipes, and we can exercise together." Chris opened the refrigerator. "I'll make you some chicken tonight, and then we can take a walk."

"No, Chris," Mia said. She bit her lower lip and stared at him. "I need you to make me do those things."

Chris sighed. Then he sat back down in the chair. "What do you mean exactly?"

"I need you to hold me accountable for this. I need your strength, your discipline, because I don't have my own."

Chris loosened his tie and became thoughtful. "I would l do anything in the world for you, Mia, but I don't know if this is a good idea."

"Why not?" Mia asked. "You're the head of our household, and you certainly aren't concerned about disciplining me for other reasons."

Chris smiled at her. "I'll do whatever it takes to keep you safe and happy."

"This is what it takes," Mia insisted.

Chris rested his chin on his hand. "This is a little bit different. I don't ever want you to think that I'm not happy with the way you look. If your doctor says you need to lose weight for your health, then I'm willing to help you do that. But you don't need to lose weight for me, Mia. I think you're beautiful just the way you are. And I don't want to give you any mixed messages about that."

Mia smiled as her heart melted inside. She had married such a wonderful man. "I know that," she said. "I know you love me. But I need to do this for me, and I can't do it without you."

Chris nodded. His chocolate brown eyes were serious. "If you're sure this is what you want, then I'll help you."

"I'm sure," Mia told him. "I need you."

"Okay, then let's make some rules," he said. "But we'll do it over dinner. I'm starved."

Mia grinned and got up to help make the chicken.

When the meal was finished, they talked about what Mia needed and what Chris could do to help her.

"I think you should keep a food diary," Chris suggested after swallowing a large piece of chicken. "We can look at it together and see what you've eaten that's not good for you."

Mia nodded. "My doctor gave me a food plan. I can't have any simple sugars or carbs like white bread or pasta."

"Okay," said Chris. He ceremoniously placed the plate of white bread on the kitchen counter. "And you should exercise at least three or four days a week."

His wife nodded. "That's what the doctor suggested."

"Then you should keep an exercise journal, too." Chris looked at Mia sympathetically. "It's not going to be easy."

"Should we have weigh-ins?" Mia asked.

Chris shook his head. "No. I'm not going to punish you based on your weight. I think that's taking things too far. But I do expect you to follow this exercise and eating plan. Got it?"

Mia nodded. "Got it."

Just as with every diet Mia had ever tried, the first week was splendid. For three days in a row, she donned her tracksuit and sneakers and set off for the park for her walk. On the fourth day, she even went by the local gym and signed up for a trial. But by the fifth day, Mia was tired. She decided to give herself a break. Then the break extended, and soon Mia realized that she'd been basically sedentary for six days.

The food plan was following the same pattern. At first Mia kept her food diary faithfully and was proud to show Chris each evening. But then her food choices started to become less and less nutritious. She was following the diet, but just barely. Then suddenly one day she lost all sense of self-control. She drove straight to the grocery store and bought an entire cheesecake, which she devoured as soon as she got home.

After the deed was done, Mia felt terrible. She couldn't believe she'd done this to herself. She knew that she could keep it from Chris if she'd wanted to, but she also knew that it wasn't going to help her at all if she did.

That evening, she approached him. He was sitting on the sofa with the television on and some work papers spread over the coffee table.

"I want to show you my food diary," she said softly.

Chris looked up. "Hm? Okay, hand it over."

She handed him the small notebook and then slumped into a chair beside him.

Chris's round, baby-face contorted into a frown as he read the diary. He was silent for a long time as he studied it.

Finally Mia could stand it no longer. "I ate an entire cheesecake!" she blurted.

"So I see," said Chris.

"And I haven't exercised in almost a week."

Chris put the notebook down on the table. "I made a promise to you, and I intend to keep it," he said evenly.

Mia shivered. "I know."

"Go on into the bedroom," said Chris. "Put on your gym clothes."

"My gym clothes?" she repeated with a frown.

Chris nodded. "Yes. Get going."

Mia hurried to the bedroom. She dug into the closet and found the green shorts and gray t-shirt she'd planned to wear to the gym. Then she added her sneakers just in case that was what Chris had wanted.

When she was dressed, Mia sat on the bed and waited. She felt the nerves that always plagued her when she was awaiting Chris's discipline. But she also felt a strange sense of comfort, and for the first time she believed she had actually found a path toward a healthy lifestyle.

7

When Chris appeared in the doorway, he looked very serious. Mia gulped.

"Stand up," Chris said. When she did, he took her by the shoulders and turned her toward the mirror. "Look at yourself," Chris told her.

Mia looked. She had made it a habit to avoid mirrors the past several years because she was ashamed of her appearance. She felt that shame now as she saw her pudgy thighs peeking out of the shorts and the rolls of fat hanging out of the sleeves of her t-shirt. She turned her eyes toward the carpet.

Chris responded with a hard smack to the seat of her shorts. "I said look at yourself."

Mia was startled by his forcefulness, but she lifted her eyes again.

"What do you see?" Chris asked her.

Mia shook her head. "I don't know, Chris. I just see me. I see plain, fat, awful me."

Chris held her firmly by the shoulders. "Look again. What do you think I see?"

Mia looked, and then she shrugged. "Failure."

Chris actually shook her a bit. "Mia, how can you think that?"

Mia blinked, and a tear rolled down her cheek.

Chris set his mouth into a firm line. "What do you think I see when I look at you?"

Mia raised her eyes and then broke into sobs. "I don't even want to think about it!"

Chris pulled her close and held her. Then he raised her chin and looked directly into her eyes. "When I look at you, I see desire. You are a sexy, beautiful woman inside and out. Every time you come into a room and give me that impish smile, I just want to carry you into the bedroom and make love to you."

Mia choked out a laugh through her tears. "You do?"

"Yes, I do," said Chris. "But now we've got something to take care of, don't we?"

His wife nodded and whispered, "Yes."

"You made a commitment to stick to a plan, and you broke that commitment. Didn't you?"

"Yes sir," Mia whispered, not making eye contact with him. She was ashamed of herself.

"Bend over the bed," Chris told her.

Only Chris and Mia knew that they had chosen this particular bed frame because the mattress came right up to Mia's waist. She bent down across the bed, her feet barely touching the ground.

She heard Chris behind her, and then she felt him rub her bottom with his strong hand. "When you don't stick to your plan, you're going to be punished in your gym clothes. I hope that when you put them on, you will be that much more motivated to follow through."

"Yes sir," Mia answered. She could feel the lump of anxiety in her throat. She hated being made to stick her bottom out into the room this way. She hated that she looked like a naughty little girl about to have her bottom spanked.

Chris raised his hand, and it fell hard onto the back of Mia's shorts. At the first swat, she jumped up. Chris pushed her back down. Then he delivered a searing spanking that she felt right through the fabric of her shorts. After only a few volleys of swats, her bottom was jiggling this way and that. She couldn't help but kick and wiggle to escape the pain.

"Ow!" she cried out. "I'm sorry! Chris please, I'm sorry!"

Chris didn't let up on the severity of the spanking. His hand fell hard and fast all over the wiggling, fabric-covered bottom. To Mia, it felt like a hot iron landing repeatedly on her backside.

"Please, Chris!" she begged. "I'm sorry!"

Chris stopped only long enough to pull down Mia's gym shorts. Her panties followed.

"Your little posterior is red already," Chris told her.

"It hurts," she whined.

"You think about that the next time you reach for cheesecake," he told her. Then he began to spank her hard on her unprotected bottom. Mia's bottom was already stinging, and this assault was horrendous. She bucked back and forth, but Chris held her down as he whacked her again and again on her bare cheeks.

Mia tears fell steadily onto the bed's plush comforter. She cried out her disappointment in herself, and she cried out her own self-loathing. Her bottom grew sore and hot, and Mia matched its intensity with her tears.

Chris stopped then and stood back to admire his work. Mia could feel her cheeks flaming with pain. She continued to cry.

"Into the corner," Chris ordered.

Mia hopped up and nearly ran to the corner of their bedroom. She stuck her nose against the wall and clasped her hands in front of her to make sure she didn't rub her bottom. Chris never allowed her to rub while she was in the corner.

"Are we going to have to repeat this, young lady?" Chris asked her.

"No sir," Mia said through her sobs.

"What are you going to do tomorrow?"

"Go to the gym," she said.

"I think you should use the stationary bikes tomorrow," Chris suggested.

Mia released a new flood of tears.

"Don't you think sitting on a stationary bike with a sore bottom will help you remember to keep your commitments in the future?"

"Yes, sir," Mia wailed.

"Good," Chris said. "And what are you going to do when you want a slice of cheesecake?"

"Um… eat some fruit?" she answered.

"That's an acceptable answer," her husband agreed. He approached her from behind and began to pat her burning bottom.

"Ouch," she gasped.

He laughed. Then he squeezed her gently and allowed his hand to roam the expanse of her bottom. "I'm going to miss this once you work it all off," he teased her.

"I promise to save some for you," she said, her tears mixing with her giggles.

Chris leaned over and began to nibble on her neck. "I want to see your food diary every evening for awhile," he said.

"Yes sir," she breathed.

"And I expect your gym visits to be every other day," he told her sternly. "I think you'll do better when you have a plan."

"I will," she promised. She leaned against him, held up by his strength.

"Now let's see about that fertility issue," he murmured, taking her hand and leading her back to the bed.

Eight weeks later, Mia turned to her husband with delight. She'd been standing in front of the mirror in her bedroom, modeling the new dress he'd bought for her. It was a full size smaller than her old dresses. She loved the way the flirty hemline swished around her legs. And she loved that her legs were getting muscular from her time at the gym.

She flew into his arms. "I love it! Thank you!"

He caught her and laughed. "The only problem is that in a few more weeks, it will be too big for you."

Mia smiled slyly. "Don't count on it," she said.

"What do you mean?" Chris looked at her quizzically.

"I'm off the diet for now," Mia announced.

"I thought you were shooting for forty pounds?"

Mia's smile lit up the whole bedroom. "That will have to wait. Right now, I'm shooting for motherhood. We're having a baby!"

The Pills

It started with a headache.

"Honey, do we have ibuprofen?" Dave called from the hallway.

Brandy stopped mid-way through folding a pair of jeans. "It's in the hall closet," she said. "You okay?"

"Just a headache," Dave answered. He poked his head around the corner of the bedroom door and grinned at her. "Is it still in that basket on the top shelf?"

"Uh huh," Brandy answered. Then she remembered something awful. She felt a jolt of anxiety catch in her throat. "I'll get it for you."

"I'll get it," Dave told her. "You're busy with the laundry."

Brandy's heart pounded as she listened to her husband's footsteps in the hallway. She heard the door squeak open and the sound of him rustling through the closet. She shut her eyes tight and waited.

Soon, Dave appeared in the doorway. This time he didn't look playful or happy. "You have something to tell me?"

Brandy put down the laundry. For half a second, she considered lying. Then she realized that it was the wrong thing to do. And anyway, it wouldn't work and would get her into more trouble than she was already in.

"They're just pills, Dave," she said, trying to calm him down.

It didn't work. Dave held the bottle out to her. "They're diet pills. And I'm willing to bet that your doctor didn't tell you to buy these."

Brandy sat on the bed. "I saw a commercial on TV, and I wanted to try them."

Dave sat beside her. "What are you thinking, Brandy? These things aren't good for you. They speed up your heart rate, and they make you crazy."

"But I need to lose twenty pounds," Brandy said, defeated.

Dave put an arm around her shoulder. "You listen to me, young lady. You are absolutely beautiful just the way you are."

"No I'm not," Brandy insisted. "I'm fat and ugly. If I don't do something about this weight gain, the day's going to come when you won't want to be married to me anymore."

Dave sighed as Brandy began to cry. He held his wife in his arms and he thought about what to do next.

Finally he lifted Brandy up beside him. "Look at me," he ordered. His voice was dark, and it had a threatening edge.

She did. Her freckled face was wet with tears.

"You don't need to lose a pound," he told her.

"But I…"

"Don't interrupt me," he commanded. "You are perfect just the way you are. You might not be as small as you used to be, but you are healthy and strong."

"I don't feel healthy and strong," Brandy muttered. "I'm a cow."

Now Dave's voice became firm. "You're going to stop that talk right this instant. I would never let anyone speak about you like that, and I am certainly not going to sit here and listen while you talk like that about yourself. Do you hear me?"

Brandy nodded. "I hear you."

"You are healthy, Brandy. Has your doctor suggested you lose weight?"

"No," she admitted.

"And you know something? Even if you were overweight, even if you were unhealthy, I would still love you. I am your husband, and I will always love you no matter what you look like," Dave told her. His face was full of concern. "And you should know that, Brandy. I'm disappointed that you don't."

"You don't want a fat wife," Brandy said with disgust.

Dave sighed and tried to control his temper. "Would you stop loving me if I gained fifty pounds?" he asked. "Or if I lost my hair?"

"It's different for men," Brandy argued. "It's not the same thing at all. If I gained fifty pounds, you'd probably head for the first young girl who looked your way."

13

"That's it," said Dave, his face flaming with anger. "I'm shocked that you would say something like that to me."

He tugged her arm and pulled her facedown over his lap.

Brandy struggled. "Hey! No, Dave!"

"You need an attitude adjustment," Dave said.

"Let me go!" Brandy yelled.

Dave answered with a volley of sharp swats to the back of Brandy's cotton dress. She twisted and wailed at the searing pain.

"You are going to stop this talk immediately," Dave commanded. He continued to spank her hard over her dress. Brandy yelled.

"And you are going to throw those pills out today!" Dave continued.

"No," said Brandy, struggling for all she was worth. "I just bought them. I don't even know if they work yet."

Dave lifted her dress off her bottom and put his large hand on her panties. He could already see her bottom turning pink under the thin, white cotton. He yanked her panties down with one motion, and she gasped.

"No, Dave," she pleaded. She was starting to lose the edge in her voice. "Please don't."

"You need this," Dave answered. He began a serious spanking, starting with alternating swats to her pink cheeks.

Brandy scissored her legs in the air and wailed. "Stop!"

Each movement Brandy made seemed to increase Dave's resolve. His spanks gained intensity until her bottom was a deep bright pink, bordering on red.

"You'd better not ever, ever, tell me again that I would cheat on you!" he told her.

"I won't!" Brandy cried. "I'm sorry!"

"You are beautiful," Dave told her as he smacked her soundly, leaving handprints as he spanked. "You are perfect just the way you are."

Brandy started to cry hard, and her legs stopped kicking. She stayed there over Dave's lap as he slapped her bare bottom with quick, sharp movements.

"You're going to throw those pills away," Dave insisted.

Brandy gasped and sobbed. "But Dave, I need them."

Dave grimaced. Then he pulled one of her legs over his own so that he had access to the underside of her bottom and the inside of her thighs.

Brandy began to panic. "No, Dave, no!"

Dave's hand landed hard on the tender under curve of Brandy's bottom, and she squealed. He repeated the motion on the other cheek, and then began to spank the tops of her thighs.

"Dave, it hurts! It hurts!" Brandy cried out.

"You are going to throw those pills out, and you are not going to buy any more ever again!" Dave said. He smacked her hard between each word and she went into hysterics.

"I will, Dave! I will! Please stop!" she cried, although it was hard to understand her words through her sobs.

Dave covered the skin under Brandy's cheeks with spanks until they were the same uniform color as the rest of her bottom while Brandy cried and wriggled all over his lap.

Then he released her so that her legs were back together, but he still held her tightly over his knees. One hand was stiff against her back, and the other rested on her sore bottom.

"You are beautiful," he told her firmly. "Repeat it."

Brandy cried louder.

Dave spanked her hard, and she lurched forward on his lap. "I am beautiful!" she wailed.

"Again!" Dave commanded, smacking her three times sharply where her bottom met her thighs.

"I am beautiful!" Brandy yelled.

"Say it again," said Dave. He was rubbing her bottom now instead of spanking it.

"I am beautiful," Brandy choked through her sobs. "I am beautiful."

"Good," said Dave. He continued to rub her bottom as her sobs subsided. He gave her a few minutes to compose herself and then pulled her up to sit on his lap. He kept a hand on her bottom while he looked her in the eye. "I will always love you, Brandy Jane Williamson. I don't care if your hair falls out and your toes turn purple. I will love you forever."

Brandy began to giggle, even as the tears streamed from her eyes, and Dave smiled. "You don't have to change a thing about yourself," he said softly.

15

Brandy buried her head in his shoulder. "I just feel so insecure sometimes," she whispered.

"If you feel insecure, then you should talk to me," said Dave. "But you are not allowed to follow any crazy diets or to put these pills in your body. Do you understand me?"

Brandy nodded against his chest. "I understand."

"And Brandy, if you do it again, I'm going to spank you harder than you've ever been spanked in your life," he told her. "And that's a promise."

Brandy snuggled up against him. "I won't. I won't do it again."

Dave kissed her on the head and held her against him. He knew that he was the luckiest man in the world to be married to Brandy, and he resolved to let her know that each and every day.

The Cut

Laura sighed deeply as she flipped through the pages of the glossy magazine. She pointed to photo of a popular celebrity who was dressed to the nines for some awards show or other. "Ooooh, look at her."

Ellie leaned across the coffee table and peered at the magazine. "Wow. That pixie cut is so in right now."

Laura nodded. "It's really cute."

"It would look terrific on you," said Ellie. "You should get one."

Laura reached back and stroked her long, strawberry blonde braid. She'd had long hair for years and was constantly braiding, brushing or washing it. She wondered what it would be like to have a cut that required less care. She shook her head. "Evan would kill me."

Ellie looked thoughtful. She knew that Laura and Evan had an old-fashioned relationship. Ellie and her husband Mark shared the same kind of marriage. The women often commiserated about the ups and downs of being married to an authoritative man.

"Maybe if you could show him the photo," Ellie suggested.

"Then I'd just get a lecture on reading these silly magazines," Laura laughed. She dropped the magazine onto the table.

"Has Evan actually said you can't cut your hair? Has he come right out and told you that?" Ellie asked slyly.

"Well, not in so many words," Laura replied. "But I know he wouldn't like it. He believes that women should have long hair. He likes me to be feminine."

"But it's your hair," Ellie argued.

Laura had to laugh at the whine in her friend's voice. "What about you? Why don't you get a short do?"

Ellie's dark hair hung just below her shoulders. She smiled. "It wouldn't look good on my pudgy face."

Laura had to grin. Ellie was a beautiful woman, but she was rather round. Her face was almost a perfect circle. Keeping her hair down below her shoulders made her features look a bit thinner.

"I bet Evan would love it if he saw it on you," Ellie said.

Laura smiled. "You think?"

Her friend nodded. "It would compliment your face so well."

Laura thought about this. Maybe Evan would like it. "I'll ask him tonight," she said.

Ellie nodded. "It can't hurt to ask," she agreed.

That night, Evan wasn't in a very good mood. He'd had a long day at work, and all he wanted was a good dinner and a long sleep. Several times, Laura almost brought up the subject of her hair only to stop short. It certainly wasn't a good idea to ask him when he was in a mood like this. Surely he'd say no to anything. She decided to sleep on it and ask him at a better time.

The next morning the phone rang at nine. Laura was still clearing the breakfast dishes. "Hello?"

It was Ellie. 'What did he say?"

"Hm?" Laura asked. She put a stack of plates into the cupboard. "About what?"

"About your hair," Ellie prompted.

"Oh," Laura said, remembering. "I didn't ask him. He was in a bad mood."

Ellie sighed loudly.

"What is it?" Laura asked.

"My stylist can take you at one," Ellie said in a rush.

Laura laughed. "No way."

"Come on," Ellie said. "It's such a cute cut, and I know he'll love it once he sees it on you."

Laura bit her lip. "I really do want to try it."

"Then try it!" Ellie said enthusiastically.

"But I can't disobey Evan," Laura replied.

"You're not disobeying Evan," Ellie reminded her. "Evan didn't say you couldn't do this."

"I didn't ask him," Laura reminded her.

"And he didn't say no," Ellie said. "Come on, we'll make a day of it. We'll go to the stylist and out to lunch. It'll be fun."

18

Laura grinned. She really did want the cut. And maybe Ellie was right. Maybe Evan would love it. "Okay, I'll do it."

The cut was stunning. Laura was thrilled when she looked into the mirror. She was absolutely glowing. After she'd come home that afternoon, she studied herself in the mirror. She knew she looked great, but she was nervous about what Evan would say. She tried to ignore the rock in her stomach as she prepped for dinner.

When Laura heard Evan's key turn in the front door, she felt a jolt of anxiety in her chest. She was nervous, yes. But what was that other feeling? Could it be guilt?

Evan entered the kitchen and stopped suddenly, his dark eyes fully open with surprise. Then he placed his keys on the counter and walked toward his wife. He kissed her hello and then held her at arm's length.

"You want to tell me about this?" he asked, raising an eyebrow.

"I cut it," Laura said in a very small voice. "Do you like it?"

Evan studied her for several seconds. Then he nodded. "It looks very nice on you," he said finally.

Laura let out her breath in a flood of relief. "I'm glad. I was worried that you wouldn't like it."

" But do you think that it's appropriate to make such a change in your appearance without asking me first?" Evan said, his voice calm but firm.

Laura's eyes slipped to the floor. "I was going to ask you," she said in her defense, "but you were in such a terrible mood last night."

"That's doesn't answer the question," Evan stated. "Do you think it's appropriate to make this decision without consulting me?"

"No sir," Laura replied in a small voice.

"What are we going to do about this, Laura?" Evan towered over her, and she felt very small.

"I don't know," she said, without meeting his eyes.

"I think you do," her husband said. "Turn around and lift your skirt."

"Here? In the kitchen?" Laura gasped.

Evan nodded solemnly. "Here in the kitchen."

Laura felt tears spring into her eyes. Evan looked very serious and very disappointed in her. She turned so that she was leaning against the counter and she slowly lifted her skirt.

She felt Evan pat her bottom through her panties. Then he pulled them down to her knees. She shivered as the air hit her bare skin.

Evan leaned in close and spoke in her ear. She could feel the heat from his breath as his words entered her consciousness. "I want you to listen carefully to me."

"Yes sir," she whispered.

Evan's hand rested on her bottom, and he gave her a little squeeze. "I am not a dictator, Laura. If you'd like to try a new hairstyle, I'm not going to forbid it. However, I do expect you to consult me on matters like this. I want to be able to discuss these decisions with you and to come to an agreement about what is right. Do you understand?"

"Yes sir," Laura repeated. She knew he was right. He would not have forbidden her to cut her hair. He would have talked to her about it, and he probably would have made her see that she really didn't want to cut her hair at all. Instead of consulting her dearest love and protector, she'd been rebellious and stubborn. "I'm sorry."

"If you had asked me, I would have suggested a style that was less drastic a change. I would have reminded you of the person you are inside and the image you want to present to the world. I would have reminded you what you yourself believe about the need for a woman to present her feminine qualities," Evan said.

"You're right, Evan," Laura answered.

"I'm glad you feel that way," Evan told her. "It makes my job easier. But you're still going to be punished, and I hope it will help you make better decisions in the future."

Laura sniffed but she didn't argue. "Yes sir," she said.

"Hand me that wooden spoon," Evan told her.

Laura's heart jumped, but she did as she was told. She reached across the counter and into the utensil jar for the large wooden cooking spoon. She handed it to Evan.

"Bottom out," Evan told her.

Laura knew what he wanted. She stuck out her bottom so that it made a better target for Evan. A sob caught in her throat and she swallowed.

Evan tapped the spoon against the lower part of Laura's bottom cheeks, and she shivered. When he spanked her with the spoon or a long paddle, he often concentrated on the curves of her bottom so that she would feel it when she sat.

20

She braced herself against the counter as she felt the airspace increase between the spoon and her bottom, and then she shut her eyes for the inevitable whack. It stung, and she cried out.

Evan repeated the action with another blow to the opposite cheek, and Laura jumped up on her toes.

"Back down and stick that bottom out, Laura," Evan ordered.

"Yes sir," she answered. Then she squealed as the spoon fell again. "It hurts."

Evan answered with a volley of swats causing Laura to jump and squeal. Each smack added a fresh sting that faded into the general pain that grew in her bottom. Evan expertly covered the entire area of Laura's lower bottom cheeks, and she began to really cry.

Evan believed that scolding Laura as she cried was the way into her heart, and he took this opportunity. "You are my wife, Laura, and you have a responsibility to discuss these decisions with me," he told her sternly. He punctuated this thought with an especially hard swat to the middle of Laura's bottom.

Laura sobbed, and Evan continued.

"You will show more maturity in the future," he said. Then he swatted her hard a second time in the same place.

Laura's knees buckled, but Evan pulled her back into position. "Do you hear me, Laura?"

"Yes sir," Laura gasped through her tears. "I'm sorry!"

Evan put the spoon down on the counter. Then he began to spank her fast and hard with his hand.

Laura's feet kicked up into the air and she began an involuntary dance. Evan held her tightly and continued the spanking.

"What are you going to do next time, Laura?" Evan asked without pausing the spanking.

"I'm... I'm going to ask you!" Laura cried out. Her feet were moving rapidly, and she was almost without the ability to control them.

"You certainly are," Evan told her. He whacked both cheeks hard several more times and then he turned her around forcefully and kissed her, pressing his lips hard against hers.

Laura's tears were still flowing freely. "I'm sorry, Evan," she cried.

Evan pulled her into his chest and let her cry. "I know you are, baby."

They stayed like this for several minutes until Laura's sobs calmed to whimpers. Then Evan tilted her chin so that she was looking into his eyes.

"How much did this haircut cost us?" he asked her.

"Ellie paid for it," she admitted. Laura hated to incriminate her friend, but she wasn't going to lie to her husband.

Evan nodded. "I had a feeling Ellie was in on this."

Laura shook her head. "It was my fault."

"Your actions were your fault, yes," Evan said. "But Mark's getting a phone call."

"No, Evan," Laura began. But a look from Evan stopped her. Her bottom still stung and she wasn't about to pursue a course of action that could very well lead to more punishment.

She watched Evan reach for the phone and dial Mark's number. Then he walked into the other room, presumably for some privacy.

Laura turned her attention back to her dinner. She was sorry that Ellie was going to get dragged into this.

After a few minutes, Evan came back into the kitchen. "Wash your face if you want to, sweetie. Ellie and Mark are coming over."

Laura was surprised. "They're coming over here?"

Evan grabbed a piece of pork directly off the stove and popped it into his mouth. "This is good," he said, as if nothing strange was happening.

They had finished their dinner by the time the doorbell rang. Laura opened the front door to a very nervous looking Ellie and a serious Mark. "Hello," she said.

"Hello, Laura," Mark studied her hair and then shook his head. He turned to his wife. "This is what you talked her into?"

Ellie nodded sheepishly. "Yes."

Laura felt the need to come to her friend's defense. "Ellie didn't talk me into it at all," she insisted. "I was the one who wanted to cut it. Ellie just..."

"Made the appointment and paid for it," Mark finished.

Ellie groaned.

"Come inside," Evan called from the living room. Ellie and Mark sat down on the sofa, and Mark stood next to Laura's armchair.

Evan got straight to the point. "Laura got her bottom spanked over this," he said evenly.

22

Laura felt her face blush bright red, and Ellie looked at the floor. "I'm sorry, Laura," she said.

"And now she understands the need to discuss these things with me," Evan continued. "But I'm still concerned about this friendship."

"I agree," Mark said. "We can't have you two acting like ten-year-old girls, pushing each other into bad behavior."

Ellie and Laura exchanged glances. This was a very accurate description of their friendship.

"So what are we going to do about this?" asked Evan. "Do you ladies have any ideas?"

Laura was terrified that the men would suggest that they spend less time together. "Evan, please don't take Ellie away from me," she pleaded.

Evan smiled at her and kissed the top of her head. "I would never do that to you, honey," he said. "We just need to find a way to keep this kind of thing from happening again."

"It won't," Ellie promised. "It won't happen again."

"It had better not," Mark said. He looked hard at his wife. "Ellie's going to feel my belt on her bare bottom when we get home. Let's hope that's sufficient motivation for her."

The color drained from Ellie's face.

"Okay," said Evan. "You girls are both getting punished, and I think you deserve another chance. But if something like this happens again, your play dates are going to have to be supervised for a while. Does that sound right, Mark?"

Mark nodded. "That sounds just right."

"Do you understand the rules, Laura? Ellie?"

Both women nodded silently.

Mark got up. "All right, young lady. Let's get home." He took Ellie's hand and pulled her to a standing position. She was about a foot shorter than her husband, and he held her hand tightly as if she were a child.

Laura said goodbye to her friend as Ellie followed Mark out the door. Then men shook hands and then Evan shut the door behind them. He put his arms around Laura. "You've got to do what's right even when your friends are telling you otherwise," he told his wife.

Laura leaned against him. "I know," she said.

He smiled at her. "Let's go to bed."

Laura followed her husband into the bedroom. Her bottom was still sore, but love for him swelled in her heart.

On the next block, Ellie had a very different feeling in the pit of her stomach. She stood in the corner of the bedroom, her nightgown pulled up in the back to reveal her soft, white bottom.

Mark was pacing behind her. "You know that you have a great deal of influence over Laura," he told her. "What I cannot understand is why you don't choose to influence her in a positive way."

Ellie bit her lip and looked at the paint on the wall in front of her. She didn't mean to influence Laura negatively. She was only trying to be a friend.

"You need to think before you speak, Eleanor," Mark said firmly. "And you need to consider that Laura believes everything you say. You have a responsibility to lead her down a proper path."

Tears formed in Ellie's eyes. She hadn't realized that she was misleading her friend. She would never pull Laura into a bad situation on purpose.

"It is inexcusable for you to encourage Laura to disobey her husband, Ellie," Mark said. "I just don't understand what got into you."

Ellie didn't understand either.

"I'm going to spank your bottom with my belt, and I want you to think about your behavior and where it leads," Mark said. "Then I think you need to spend some time over my knee to help you remember just who is in charge in this marriage."

Ellie grimaced. This didn't sound good for her at all.

"Keep that nightgown up and away from your bottom," Mark commanded.

Ellie pulled the nightgown up to her waist. Her ample bottom was bare and ready. She winced as she heard him unbuckle his belt and pull it from the loops.

She heard him double the strap of leather in his hands, and she felt his presence beside her. He slid his arm around her waist and held her firmly in his grasp.

Ellie yelped as the belt cracked across her cheeks.

The swats came hard and fast, steadily covering Ellie's entire bottom. She began to wiggle and slide away as the belt fell again and again. Mark renewed his grasp and continued the spanking.

"Your bottom is going to be red tonight," Mark informed her. He smacked her hard across the center of her bottom.

She yelped again and then broke down into hard crying. Mark continued the spanking. By the time he was finished, the belt had visited every part of Ellie's bottom three or four times.

Ellie's crying was bordering on hysterical when Mark finally pulled away from her. "Keep that nightgown up, and stay in the corner," he told her firmly.

Ellie cried into the wall as Mark moved toward the bed. He watched her there, her bottom flaming, until she calmed herself. Then he called her over to him.

"Come here, Eleanor," he ordered. His voice was still sharp.

Ellie shuffled slowly toward him. Her eyes were red and swollen.

"Over my knee," said Mark. He grabbed her hand and gently pulled her down across his lap.

Ellie's tears began to flow again when she found herself bottom up over his lap. "Please, Mark," she pleaded. "My bottom already hurts."

"Whose in charge of this relationship?" he asked. He patted her red bottom, and she squirmed.

"You are," she said, fighting a losing battle with her tears. "You're in charge."

"Do I allow you to be a bad influence on your friends?" he asked her.

"No," she cried. She felt the tears roll down her nose and splash onto the carpet.

"You're going to get a spanking on your sore bottom, Ellie, and it's going to hurt," he told her. "I want you to remember this feeling the next time you're with Laura and you two start to make your plans. I want you to remember what your bottom feels like when you lead her astray."

Ellie cried hard as Mark's hand slapped against her bottom. She knew that the spanks weren't especially hard, but they were unbearable on her already punished bottom. Mark kept one hand firmly on her back as Ellie kicked her legs and tried to swim off of his lap.

Mark continued a steady rain of slaps against Ellie's bottom, watching the dark red get even darker each time his palm fell against it. He finished with three sharp smacks to the crease between her bottom and her thigh, one on each side and one right in the middle.

Ellie fell limp over his lap at this last assault, and Mark slowly rubbed her glowing bottom.

"You're my beautiful girl, Ellie," Mark said softly. "I love you too much to let you behave that way."

Ellie couldn't answer. The tears were coming too fast. She let herself relax over Mark's lap and felt his hand rubbing gently against her bottom.

Soon Mark turned her over and began to kiss her softly on the mouth. "I love you so much," he told her.

Ellie melted into the authoritative attention of her husband, and the two of them experienced a wonderful night together.

The "Seasons" Stories

Winter Games

Kelly closed her eyes and plastered herself against the wall as the school bell rang to announce the end of the day at Baylor Christian School. There was a moment of silence followed by a massive flurry of activity, as explosive as if someone had set off a bomb. Her eyes flew open.

Children seemed to fly at her from everywhere. They poured from classrooms and crowded the hallway. The sound of lockers slamming and kids yelling filled spaces that had just been empty. She watched the kids pull on coats and hats, most of them flapping unzipped or unbuttoned because there were no mothers here to complain.

"Hey!" she called to a kid in knee-length shorts. "It's freezing out there!"

The kid grinned and flashed her a thumbs-up. She smiled back.

The halls emptied almost as quickly as they had filled. A few students remained, strolling in small groups to one after-school activity or anther. She walked down the hall until she came to Room 12B. The door was solid, tan wood with just a small strip of a glass window. She peered inside, and her heart melted at the sight of her husband.

He wore the gray pants and sweater she'd bought him for Christmas. He perched easily on his typical teacher's desk, a solid block of light-colored wood. As he leaned forward a piece of his dark hair feel onto one of the lenses of his charming, silver-rimmed glasses.

28

She nearly went weak in the knees with love for him.

She knocked on the door. He turned his head toward her and smiled. Then he made a beckoning motion with his hand. She opened the door and came inside.

"Hello darling," he said. "What are you doing here?"

She shrugged and gave him a flirty grin. "I was on my way home from the hospital. The bus stops here, so I thought I'd get a ride from you."

Kelly worked as a Nurse's Aid at the local children's hospital. She was picking up shifts for extra money wherever she could get them, and her schedule was completely disorganized. She didn't mind though. She kind of liked a hectic lifestyle, and it wasn't as if they had children. Besides, this was how she and Marshall worked best. She was spontaneous and creative, and he was steady and organized.

Marshall addressed the pair of boys who sat side-by-side in desks in front of him. "Alex and Bradley, this is my wife Mrs. Hammond."

Kelly smiled broadly. They had only been married since summer, and hearing her new name still gave her a thrill.

"Hello Mrs. Hammond," the boys chorused dutifully. They were both slumped in their desks, and it was obvious that Marshall had kept them after school. She recognized their names as two of his kids who suffered behavioral challenges. She always laughed when Marshall told her that. She herself had been considered a behavioral challenge when she was in the sixth grade, just like these boys were. She knew now that it was only because she wasn't able to sit still as long as was required for school.

Marshall had teased her. "If you were in my class, I'd spank your behind."

She had only laughed. Now she looked at the two boys with sympathy. "Aw Marsh," she said. "Let 'em go. It's Friday."

The kids giggled at the use of this nickname for their teacher. Then they looked up at Marshall expectantly.

He coughed and shot his wife a look of disapproval. Then he turned back to the boys. "Lucky for you, I have papers to grade. You can go this time. But if it happens again, you are in my detention for an entire hour. Are we clear?"

"Yes sir," said Alex. Bradley repeated this. Then they were out the door so fast that Kelly only saw a streak.

Marshall stood up and closed the door behind the boys. Then he turned to his wife and gave her a quick kiss. "So you came over to disrupt the discipline of my classroom?"

She laughed at his teasing. "Are you ready to go?"

Marshall glanced at his desk. "I really do have some work to do," he said. "Can you give me half an hour?"

She nodded. "Yep. I'll wait in the hallway?"

"Good," he said. "Check out the teacher's lounge. There's a new coffee maker."

"Oooh," said Kelly. "Sounds fancy."

"Don't make fun," he said. "At least this one gives liquid."

She kissed him again and left him to his papers. "Don't be long," she told him.

He blew her a kiss as she walked out the door, and her knees went weak again.

She looked down the hallway to her right and then to her left, thinking about how to entertain herself for the next half hour. She certainly wasn't interested in the new coffee machine.

She headed toward the front of the school and looked out the window. Snow covered the ground like a fuzzy layer of pillow stuffing. She turned to the parking lot and saw Marshall's two delinquents standing in the snow with some other kids.

She pulled her hat down low over her ears so that her blonde curls stuck out underneath. Then she buttoned up her pea coat. She'd changed into jeans before leaving work. The scrubs were just too cold for the icy wind. Wrapped up tight, she headed outside.

The air was brisk, and the cold filled her nose as she breathed. She waved to the kids as she approached. "Hey!"

"Hey," Alex returned the greeting. "So that was pretty cool in there."

She flashed him a bright smile. "I know how it is," she said. "I got detention a lot."

"And you married Hammond?" the boy demanded. "That must be like detention all the time!"

Bradley looked a little stunned, but Kelly laughed loudly at the boy's joke. "So what are you guys doing?"

"Snowballs," said a smaller boy who stood behind Alex. "Wanna throw some?"

"Yeah!" said Kelly eagerly. "What are we throwing them at?"

All the boys laughed. "We were having a fight," said Bradley. He pointed to a large pile of snow by the entrance of the parking lot. "There's one of the forts, but the other one crashed."

"The Lobster ran into it," Alex explained glumly.

"I did not!" protested a child with fierce red hair and freckles.

"You fell right on top of it," Bradley said. "So now we're tossing them at cars."

Kelly nodded. It made perfect sense to her. "Count me in," she said.

Alex looked her up and down. "You got snow pants?"

"Nope," Kelly answered. "Do I need them?"

The boy shrugged. "Not if you don't mind getting wet."

Kelly joined the troop behind their fort. She couldn't contain her joy as she knelt behind the sturdy wall of snow. She could feel the cold flow off the white paradise and collide with her warm breath.

She and Alex made snowballs furiously until the first car came around the corner. Bradley picked one up and slammed it into the passenger door, where it smashed into a thousand little pieces.

"If someone gets out of their car, you should run," Alex instructed, crunching a snowball between his gloves.

Kelly was concerned. "Why? We're not damaging anything."

"People get weird," said Alex with a shrug. He leaned over and demonstrated his snowball technique to Kelly. "You've got to pack it tight. Yours are going to fall apart in the air."

They continued this way for quite a while, watching as Bradley expertly aimed his snowballs at passing cars. Most of the drivers never even knew they'd been hit. The snowballs tended to flatten themselves against a tire or a back door.

"You try one," Bradley said to Kelly.

Kelly grinned. "I'm not that good at throwing."

"Just close your eyes and let it fly," the boy advised. "If you miss, it's no big deal."

Kelly nodded. She picked up a neat, tight snowball.

"Here's one!" said Bradley, pointing toward the parking lot.

Kelly did as she'd been instructed. She closed her eyes, and she let it fly.

There was a collective gasp from the group of boys. Then Alex said, "Run!"

Kelly opened her eyes to disaster. Her snowball had flown into

31

Marshall's car. It had sailed right to the driver's side window. And unfortunately for Marshall, the window had been open.

Marshall pulled his car over and got out, wiping snow from his eyes. He thundered toward Kelly. "What on earth is going on here?"

She turned around and saw her newfound friends running through the snow as fast as their legs could carry them. She turned back to her husband. He looked very angry and very wet. She suppressed a giggle.

"Hi honey," she said.

"Kelly…" Marshall began. He took a deep breath. "What are you doing?"

She smiled weakly. "The kids and I were just throwing some snowballs."

"At cars?"

"Well yes," she said. "It didn't seem like it could hurt anything."

Marshall folded his arms across his taupe overcoat. "I was looking for you."

"I guess I lost track of time," she said.

"Playing in the snow," Marshall grumbled.

"I didn't mean to hit you, Marsh," she said. Then she couldn't stop herself. The hilarity of her new husband standing in front of her with snow dripping down his face was just too much. She burst out laughing.

Marshall's face turned red. Then he grabbed his wife and tossed her over his shoulder.

"Marshall!" Kelly screeched. "What are you doing?"

Marshall slapped the back of her jeans, and Kelly screeched. "We're going home," Marshall told her. "And we're going to talk about this."

He deposited her in the car, and she could still feel the sting from the smack he'd given her. She looked out the window as they drove away, and she caught site of Alex waving to her from across the schoolyard. Sheepishly she waved back.

He didn't speak to her until they pulled into the driveway. She kept quiet, too, because she wasn't sure what to say.

"Get in the house," Marshall told her firmly. She hopped out of the car and scurried up to the door where she let herself in. Her husband followed her.

As soon as they were in the living room, he began to talk. "Kelly Jo, of all the childish, immature behavior…"

Kelly Jo? She grimaced. This was not going to be good.

He stopped. "Take off your coat."

She peeled off her coat and then offered Marshall an apologetic smile as the snow fell in clumps onto the carpet. She took off her hat and let her wild hair fall around her face in unruly curls. Her jeans were wet from sitting on the cold, snowy ground.

"I'm wet," she said.

"I can see that," Marshall told her. "Take them off. You aren't going to need them."

She looked up at him in shock. "Take them off?" she repeated. "Here?"

"Here," he told her.

She undid the button and then the zipper. Then she pushed the jeans down to her knees and pulled them off one leg at a time. She stood there in pink striped panties. They were wet and cold, too.

"I could throw these in the wash," she said.

"Just put them down," Marshall told her. "Are your panties wet too?"

She nodded.

He took a step toward her. Then he grabbed her by the arm, sat down on the sofa and pulled her across his lap in one fluid motion.

She fought. She kicked, and she clawed but she didn't go anywhere. Marshall had her down.

He whacked her hard on the back of her damp panties. She felt a sting like the one from the parking lot, only several times more intense. "Ouch!" she cried.

"This is what happens when you act like a naughty little girl, Kelly," he told her furiously. He smacked her hard and fast on her panties. She wiggled with abandon, her legs flailing up and down.

"Marsh, stop!" she cried out as she slapped her bottom mercilessly. "Stop!"

"I am a school teacher, Kelly Jo!" he told her forcefully. He swatted her again, hard, right where her bottom and thighs met. She felt the smack like a hot iron striking her skin. "In a Christian school!" These last words he emphasized with firm spanks to her bottom cheeks.

"I know!" she yelled, her words turning into sobs somewhere between her throat and her mouth.

"I need to be married to an adult, not a child," he told her.

She let her head fall onto the sofa cushion, and she cried into the fabric.

"I do not want to be called into the principal's office Monday morning to be told that my wife was seen throwing snowballs at cars in the parking lot!" he said, each word adding force to his spanks.

Kelly felt like her bottom was going to explode. She also began to feel remorse for what she'd done. She hadn't thought about what her actions might mean to Marshall's career.

She tried to apologize, but she was crying too hard.

Marshall let loose with a flurry of swats that left Kelly nearly dizzy. Then suddenly he picked her up and stood her in front of him. He held her by the shoulders and looked into her teary, blue eyes.

She gasped and coughed and then finally her tears became silent.

"Your behavior is unacceptable," Marshall told her in his best teacher voice. "In the future, you've got to think before you act."

Kelly nodded. "I'm sorry."

"Good," Marshall stood. "You're not a little girl, Kel. You know better."

She nodded again. She did know better. She threw her arms around him and buried her head in his chest. She realized then that he was still wearing his coat. "I'm sorry!" she wailed.

He held her tightly, and then she felt his arms relax around her. "Maybe you are a little girl after all."

"Just sometimes," she said.

"And I know exactly how to handle those sometimes," he told her. He kissed her deeply.

She settled herself into his arms again. She knew this wouldn't be the last time she would find herself with a spanked bottom and a warm heart. But she knew without a doubt that this teacher she had married was exactly what she needed.

"Have you learned something?" Marshall asked her quietly.

"I learned how to make a decent snowball," she whispered.

Spring Bunny

Kay twirled in front of the mirror just one final time. She loved the way her skirt swished out around her legs. She grinned at herself, feeling a little bit silly at taking pleasure in something so childish.

"We're going to be late!" she heard her husband call from down the stairs.

"Coming!" she sang. She looked at her reflection and smiled. The Easter dress she'd chosen was perfect. It was a happy, pastel pink with a white sash around the middle and a full skirt. She'd known it was just the right dress when she saw it in the store window. She was especially sure when she saw that it was on sale.

Hearing Phillip's frustrated sigh, she bopped down the stairs and into the front hallway. The dress made her feel light and fluffy, like marshmallow candy.

"You know how crowded the service is Easter morning," said Phillip. He looked absolutely dashing in his dark suit. "I don't want to be late."

She nodded and grabbed her purse. "I'm ready."

He opened the front door for her and then stopped. He grinned. "You look beautiful," he said.

Kay beamed. "Thank you."

He slapped her on the bottom as she made her way out the door. "Now let's go!"

Kay pulled the passenger side shade down and checked herself in the mirror. Her light brown bob curled just right around her ears. She began to chatter to Phillip. "I can't wait for the egg hunt after the service," she said. She and Phillip were both Sunday School volunteers, and they'd worked on the Easter festivities together.

"Marcy is going to make a great Easter Bunny!" she chirped cheerfully. Marcy was her best friend and close confidante. Kay had helped her pick up her bunny costume the day before. Marcy was terrific with kids, and Kay knew that the day would be a success.

"Marcy's great at hippity hopping," Phillip agreed with a grin.

Kay giggled. "Well she's certainly better than the bunny from last year. When I think about that awful Tracy Grady, I just shiver. You know who she's dating now, don't you?"

"Kay," Phillip said in warning tone. "Didn't we just talk about this?"

She slumped back in her seat, adolescent style. "What?"

"Gossip," said Phillip. "That's a bad habit with you, and you have got to get it under control."

She sighed. She had agreed with Phillip when he pointed out that she was doing too much gossiping, especially about people from church. But when it came to Tracy, all boundaries went flying out the window.

"Tracy is part of your church family," Phillip reminded her. "I expect you to be kind to her whether you like her or not."

"Well I don't," Kay huffed.

Phillip opened his mouth to say something, but then he closed it again.

"Anyway, it's not gossip if it's true," Kay argued.

"It most certainly is," Phillip told her. "And you're acting like a fifteen-year-old girl instead of a thirty-five-year-old woman."

Kay made a face. She wished Marcy was with them. She would understand.

"We can settle this another way," Phillip told her, reminding her of their conversation. "You can take a break from Marcy."

Kay's heart jumped. Phillip had threatened her with confinement from her best friend for two weeks. "No. I'll try harder."

"Or we can handle it the way we handled the incident with Mrs. Fleming."

Kay stopped herself just before her eyes rolled up into her head. The incident Phillip was referring to was when their elderly neighbor was behaving like a know-it-all snoop. Kay had simply given her something to snoop about, parading around open windows in her lingerie. She hadn't meant to upset the old woman that much. Anyway, the ambulance driver had said it wasn't a heart attack.

That incident had been settled with Kay upturned over her husband's lap getting her bottom paddled.

She blushed. "I don't think that's a good idea."

"Then control yourself," Phillip said in a deep voice as he pulled the old Honda into a free parking space.

The service was beautiful. The choir was amazing, and the minister was eloquent as usual. Kay practically soared through the halls as she headed for the Sunday School materials closet.

"Let's see," she said out loud. "I put the candy in here. And the plastic eggs are in the first grade classroom."

"Have you seen Marcy?" Phillip asked.

Kay stopped walking and thought. "Now that I think of it, I haven't seen her. But the church was so crowded. I'm sure she's here somewhere."

"I'm going to check the auditorium," said Phillip. He kissed his wife lightly. "I'll meet you outside."

Kay waved as he left. The she opened the supply closet, talking to herself. "Now where was that candy? I hope the chocolate didn't melt."

When Kay finally had her eggs together, she went out onto the huge front lawn of the church. Excited children ran everywhere, waving their baskets wildly. Kay grinned at them. She loved to see the kids all fixed up in sweet little dresses and pants. There were even some ties in the bunch.

She began to poke signs into the ground, indicating which group would be hunting in which area. "I need the over 10s!" she called out. Several of the older kids came over to where she was standing. She passed out the eggs. "Under fives will hunt on this side of the church," she said, "so make those pretty easy to find."

The big kids scampered to hide their eggs. Kay laughed as she watched them so intent on their tasks. The little kids had been rounded up for cupcakes before the big hunt.

Kay heard something in the grass behind her. She turned around and laughed. There was Marcy in her full bunny costume. The big floppy ears and the pink smile were incredible.

"You look terrific!" Kay exclaimed. She ran over to her friend. "The kids are going to love you! Just let them finish the cupcakes, and we'll get started."

They stood together and watched the children eat. Kay wrinkled her nose as she saw a familiar figure passing out tiny cups of apple juice. "There's Tracy," she said, shaking her head. "Can you believe she's seeing Andy's brother? I mean, his brother! Come on."

She watched the young woman move between tables. "And where did she get that dress? Can you say inappropriate?"

Kay looked at her friend. She was surprised that Marcy wasn't saying anything. Usually she had plenty to add about Tracy. "Is it hard to talk in there?" she asked.

"Meet me in the third grade classroom after the hunt," said the Easter Bunny in a voice was that definitely not Marcy.

Kay's eyes grew wide. Her voice was a squeak. "Phillip?"

"That's Mr. Bunny to you," said Phillip, his voice muffled by the giant rabbit head. Then he hopped away, leaving her stunned.

After a very successful egg hunt, Kay stood in the third grade classroom and waited for her husband. She paced back and forth, biting her lower lip as her feelings flipped between frightened anticipation and anger. Surely this was entrapment?

She was tapping her strappy high heel on the tile floor when the bunny himself came into the room.

As he entered, he flipped off the front part of the mask. He still had giant ears, but she could see his face. He closed the door behind him, and Kay shivered when she heard the lock click.

"What happened?" she demanded.

He raised his eyebrows at her. "Excuse me?"

She softened. "Sorry. I mean, what happened to Marcy?"

"Marcy is sick," Phillip explained. "She left a message on my cell phone. But I don't want to talk about Marcy. You know what I want to talk about."

The bunny approached, and Kay backed up until she hit the windows. "You and I have something to settle."

"Phil, this isn't fair," Kay argued. "I thought you were Marcy!"

"So it's okay if you gossip behind my back?" Phillip asked her. His eyes were growing hard. Even in the bunny suit, he looked threatening.

"No, I mean… I didn't know it was you!"

"Kay, that's not the point!" Phillip snapped. "You need to stop this, and you need to stop it now. You need to stop being so mean-spirited toward Tracy, and you need to stop the gossip completely. Am I making myself clear?"

38

"You are making yourself clear," Kay repeated in an exasperated tone. She felt like screaming at him.

"That's it," he said. "There's only one way to make you understand."

Phillip grabbed a plastic chair and placed it in front of Kay. He seated himself, his furry tail sticking out the back, and flipped Kay over his knee.

"I am going to get through to you one way or another," he told her, a furry paw holding her prisoner on a fuzzy thigh.

"Phillip," she managed to shriek in a whisper. "We're at church!"

"I don't think God would have any problem with this," Phillip growled. "In fact, I think He would be all for it."

Kay gasped as the paw landed squarely on the back of her dress and sent a spark of pain through her body. "Ow!"

"Guess this rabbit's foot's not so lucky for you," Phillip said, whacking her again.

Kay groaned loudly, and not just because of his terrible joke. It hurt. It hurt a lot. The huge costumed hand was like a paddle falling against her bottom. She wiggled for all she was worth.

"If you continue this gossiping habit, I'm going to develop a habit of spanking," Phillip said. He smacked her bottom, and she flew forward on his lap.

Kay wailed. Then she shut her mouth quickly. She was worried that people outside could hear. Then she began to cry. "I'll stop, Phil. I will."

Phillip didn't answer. He just spanked her harder.

"I'll stop!" she cried. "I'll try harder!"

The paw whacked her bottom steadily, covering both cheeks at once. Kay began to feel desperation creep into her chest. She didn't know how to make this stop. Tears soaked her face.

"Phil, please!" she begged.

He smacked her a few more times and then rested his hand lazily on her backside.

"It stings," she said, more tears falling.

"It should," he told her. "I want you to apologize to Tracy."

"Noooo!" she wailed, color rising to her cheeks at the mere thought of such embarrassment. "I can't!"

Phillip whacked her hard six more times, sending her into hysterics.

"Stop! Stop! Stop!" she cried. Her bottom was beginning to feel as if it were sunburned.

"You are going to apologize to Tracy," Phillip said firmly. He punctuated this statement with a particularly brutal spank.

"I will!" Kay yelled finally. "I will! Just stop!"

"You'd better," Phillip told her. "If you don't, I'll spank you again. And I'll invite Tracy to watch!"

Kay almost choked on her tears. "I will!" she said, with more determination this time. "I'll do it right now!"

"That's better," said Phillip. He lifted a paw so that she could climb up off his lap.

Kay rubbed her bottom and regarded her husband.

He nodded toward the door. "Go ahead."

She looked at him through her tears, and she could tell that he was not about to budge. So she turned and walked through the classroom door.

Her first stop was the ladies room where she splashed water on her face and stood looking at her eyes until it was no longer obvious that she'd been crying. She glanced at the full-length mirror next to her. In her reflection she saw an unusually pretty woman in a pale pink dress. She smiled. Then she turned so that her bottom was visible in the glass. Quickly, she lifted the back of her skirt.

She sighed at what she revealed. Her bottom glowed red right through the thin fabric of her white, cotton panties.

If Tracy knew about this, Kay was sure that she would die of the embarrassment. She squared her shoulders, plastered a smile on her face and went out to find her nemesis.

Tracy stood next to a group of young girls out on the church lawn. She was laughing with them about the contents of their baskets.

"Um... Tracy?" Kay said.

Tracy looked up in surprise. "Hi Kay," she said cautiously. She knew how Kay and Marcy felt about her.

"Can I talk to you?"

Tracy nodded and followed Kay a few feet away from the group.

"Tracy, I have to tell you something," Kay said in an almost whispered rush. "I was gossiping about you, and that's not right. I'm really sorry."

Tracy was silent for several seconds while Kay stared at the ground. She spotted an Easter egg no one had picked up.

40

"I've gossiped about you, too," Tracy said finally.

"You have?" Kay asked. She was surprised only because she didn't know that Tracy knew enough about her to gossip.

Tracy nodded. "I'm sorry about that."

"Okay," said Kay. "That's good. Maybe we can start over."

Tracy was about to respond when Kay felt a small hand tugging at her dress.

She turned around to see three-year-old Emma Hansen staring up at her with large, blue eyes. Her sisters, five and seven years old, stood behind her. They were all dressed in full, yellow skirts.

"Miss Kay," said Emma's tiny voice. "Escuze me, Miss Kay."

Kay smiled down at the child. "What is it, sweetheart?"

The child's eyes held concern. "Miss Kay, are you all better? You can have one-a my chockite eggs."

Kay raised her eyebrows and felt a flutter in her stomach. "Emma, honey, what are you talking about?"

Anna, the oldest Hansen daughter, spoke up. "We were looking for more Easter eggs, and we heard something by the window. We went to see what it was and… and…"

Kay's heart fell into her stomach.

Maddie, the middle Hansen daughter could hold it in no longer. "We saw the Easter Bunny 'pank you, Miss Kay!"

Summer Swimming

The old camper rumbled along the gravel road as the family pulled into the campground. Nina Lawrence pushed her strawberry blonde bangs off her sweaty forehead and grinned at her husband. "We're here!"

"I hafta go to the bathroom!" a voice wailed from the back seat of the truck. Nina turned to her 10-year-old daughter, Tricia. The pig-tailed child was leaning forward so that she could look at her parents between the front seats.

"Oh you always have to go to the bathroom," said her 12-year-old brother in disgust.

"Trevor, I do not!" Tricia protested.

Nina sighed, and John pulled the truck in front of the campground office. "Why don't you take the kids inside?" John said. "I'll get us settled and meet you over at the camp site. I think we're in number 15 again this year."

Nina nodded appreciatively and hustled the children from the warm car. It was a hot July day, and the sun beat down on them like a spotlight. She put an arm around her daughter, who snuggled into her mother's side. Nina smiled. She was glad Tricia was still up for an occasional cuddle. If she tried anything like that with Trevor, he complained for days.

By the time Nina and Tricia got to the door, Trevor was already inside the office's small convenience store. Nina watched him looking over a selection of candy bars. He turned to her, and she shook her head. "Maybe after dinner."

Trevor sighed but knew better than to grumble. Nina was proud that her children were the most well behaved kids she knew. Most of that was due to John's influence, she was sure, but it still made her feel good as a mother. She was especially proud of them when she watched the way other children whined and fussed at their parents. There were even kids in Tricia's third-grade class who were known to pitch a tantrum like a three-year-old. Nina always smiled to herself when she encountered this type of behavior. She was a mother who truly enjoyed her children, and she was thankful for that.

She watched for Tricia to come out of the bathroom in her daisy print shorts and matching t-shirt. Sure enough, her daughter emerged a few moments later looking much more comfortable than she had been before.

"Can we have a soda?" Tricia asked her mother.

Trevor looked at her hopefully.

"You've had too much soda on this trip," Nina answered. "But you can each have a lemonade. And since you're both such great kids, you can choose a candy bar." She looked pointedly at her son. "That's for after dinner."

Trevor cheered, and Tricia gave her a hug. Then the two went off to find their treasures. When they had made their selections, Nina paid for the food. Then they all set off to find John.

He was easily found, hooking the camper up to the various required amenities. He grinned as his family approached.

"Let's go for a walk," he said to Nina.

She looked at the camper. "Don't you have a lot to do?"

He nodded and kissed her on top of her head. She smiled as she felt his unshaven face tickle her skin. "I've been driving all day. I want a break. Besides, Bob said they've opened that swimming hole by the lake. I want to take a look."

The children immediately began hopping around their parents like crazed Chihuahuas. "Daddy, can we swim? Can we swim? Please?"

"There will be plenty of time for swimming this week," their father said. "For now let's just look. We'll swim tomorrow."

The kids accepted this announcement and scampered toward the hiking path in front of their parents. John slipped his hand over Nina's as they walked. Nina loved the feeling of John's large hand holding her own. It made her feel protected and loved.

"When did they open the swimming hole?" she asked, trying to hide the enthusiasm in her voice. She loved swimming almost as much as the kids loved it, and the lake had been closed to swimming for the past two summers.

"Just this season," John answered. "And they're already having trouble with people diving from the rocks. Some people never learn."

Nina crumpled her brow. "Is that why it was closed?" she asked.

John nodded solemnly. "A child was paralyzed," he told her.

"Oh John, please don't tell the kids that," she said to him, trying to push the tragic image from her mind. She didn't want her children to have to think about something so awful.

"I won't," John agreed, "as long as I believe they will obey the rules."

"You know they will," Nina said. "They're great kids."

They approached their children who had found the swimming hole and were standing side by side, mouths open. Their eyes were fixed on three teenage boys who were taking turns diving from the tall rocks above the water. Nina found herself mesmerized as one young man climbed to the top of the rock and then did a perfect swan dive down into the rippled lake. Nina had been a competitive diver in school, and she knew the freedom of flying toward the water. "That was beautiful," she said.

"And completely dangerous," John said firmly. "Trev! Tricia! Come over here!"

The kids tore themselves away from the splendid sight and made their way to their parents.

"Did you see that, Dad?" Trevor asked, nearly vibrating with excitement. "That guy dove right off the rock. It must be thirty feet down!"

"Yeah Daddy. That was so cool!" Tricia chimed in, her little feet wiggling with pleasure in hot pink waterproof sandals. "Can we do that, Daddy? Can we?"

John folded his arms and looked into the eager faces of his children. "Absolutely not," he said.

Trevor showed instant disappointment.

Tricia said, "But Daddy…." The look on her father's face stopped her mid-sentence.

Nina saw Trevor close his mouth and then dart his eyes toward the lake. She had seen this look before, and she knew what he was

44

thinking. He knew that there would be times when he was left alone at the campground, and he believed that his parents were overprotective. She could see on his face that he was planning to dive when no one was around to stop him. She looked at John. He noticed, too.

"Trevor, Tricia, listen up," said John. He looked down at his children, his expression serious. "Diving from those rocks is against campground rules, and it is against my rules. It is very, very dangerous."

Nina and John exchanged a glance. She silently asked him not to tell the children about the tragedy, and he silently assured her that he would not.

He looked back at the kids. "If I catch either one of you on that rock, whether you dive off or not, I will blister your butt. Do you hear me?"

The kids' eyes were wide with attention. Tricia nodded slowly, and Trevor sighed. They were no strangers to spankings, but it was rare to hear their father speak so forcefully.

"Trevor?" John looked at his son. "Hear me?"

"Yes sir," Trevor answered.

Nina saw John deciding to add to the severity of the penalty for disobedience, just in case Trevor weighed the consequences and found the risk low. "And after I spank the daylights out of you, you will not be allowed to go swimming for the rest of the summer."

"The whole summer?" Tricia gasped. "Even after we go home?"

"That's right," said John. "Understand?"

The kids nodded solemnly, and John was convinced that he'd made his point. He relaxed and put an arm on Tricia's shoulder. "I just don't want to see you get hurt."

"And you can swim all you want," Nina said. "Just no diving. Okay?"

The kids agreed, and the family went back to their camper to fix dinner and enjoy the first evening of their vacation.

Two days later, Nina sat alone at the little table in front of the camper. It was early morning, and her family hadn't gotten out of bed. She liked this time as the sun was just coming up and the world was still. She sipped her coffee and breathed in the fresh air. She looked up when she heard the camper's screen door open and then shut. John came up behind her and put his large hands on her shoulders.

"Morning, baby," he said.

She smiled up at him, love for her husband washing over her. "Coffee?"

John sat in the folding chair beside her. His long legs brought his knees almost up to his chest. "Love some," he said, accepting the mug she offered.

"What's on the agenda today?" Nina asked him.

"I promised Trevor we could rent bikes and explore the trail," John said. "You want to go?"

Nina smiled. "I wouldn't mind some childless time," she said, "if you're offering."

"I am," John told her. "I'll take the kids for the morning and we'll get lunch at that place by the dock. You can just relax."

She grinned at her husband and pulled her knees up onto the chair and underneath her. She liked to fold herself into her warm robe on these chilly mornings. John wore pajama bottoms and a t-shirt. He unfolded his long body and stood.

"I'll get the kids up," he said, giving her a quick kiss as he turned to go.

She followed him inside to help get the kids ready for their excursion. It took twenty minutes to find Tricia's sneakers, and then Trevor couldn't seem to locate his water bottle. But soon enough they were all dressed and fed and ready to go. She waved as the threesome headed off toward the dock where bikes could be rented.

Once she was alone, she gave herself a little hug and tried to decide what to do with this free morning. It certainly was a gift to have time to herself. She peered outside at the kids' swimsuits hanging up on a clothesline, and she grinned. She hadn't had a chance to swim without the two sets of legs kicking around her and two high-pitched voices calling out for her to watch the newest tricks. She grabbed her swimsuit bottoms and pulled on a rash guard. She was past the time in her life where she felt comfortable in a two-piece but the scuba top with the full-cut bikini bottoms gave her just the right amount of coverage. She grabbed her towel and headed off to the swimming hole.

She was surprised to find that she was the only one there. Each time she had visited with the children, there had been at least five or six other campers enjoying the cool water. But then she reminded herself that she had only gone in the afternoon, and it was still early morning. Most people weren't ready to swim at this time of day.

She tossed her towel onto a nearby tree branch and waded in. The water swirled around her, and she felt alive in the beauty of

46

nature. She floated on her back for a little while and then swam across the length of the swimming area and back again. It felt good to stretch her body in long, elastic strokes. She could feel her muscles working together like they had in high school. She remembered what it was like to be strong and confident, perching on the blocks as she waited to slice into the water at a swim meet. She remembered the triumphant feeling of climbing the tall ladder to the highest diving board and then executing a flawless dive.

She looked up at the rock where the boys had jumped. Then she swam over to the area where they had landed. She pushed herself down under the water in order to see how deep it was. It was certainly deeper than five feet and three inches, because that's how tall Nina was. She thought for a moment, glancing from the rock to the path that led to the campground. She thought about the child that had been paralyzed. John hadn't said if it was a boy or a girl. But Nina wasn't a child. She was a grown woman, and she had a background in diving. She knew enough to jump away from the rocks and to angle her body so that she could pop up out of the water even if it was relatively shallow.

She thought of her own children, and suddenly she felt very old. She longed for the feeling of freedom she'd had as a teenager. She wanted to fly again.

She willed herself not to think about what she was doing as she climbed out of the water and made her way to the rock. She placed a bare foot on the wet stone, and she felt herself slip. She grabbed a nearby tree limb with one hand and hoisted herself up onto the first ledge. From there, she crept easily to the top.

It was a long way down, but Nina could see the waves in the lake water below. Her whole body longed to dive into the fresh wetness. She took a deep breath and then bounced on her toes as if on a diving board. Then with a bend of her knees, she stretched her arms out away from herself and then in front of her. She leapt, headfirst into the air.

The water made a soft splash as Nina glided into it with the precision of an electric knife. She came to the surface, her face shining.

Then she saw him.

He stood next to the branch where her towel still hung. His face was stunned, and his eyes were dark.

47

For a crazy moment, Nina considered swimming away. But she realized that she would have to come out of the water eventually. She took a deep breath and swam to the surface to face her husband.

As she pulled herself up out of the water, her body dripped. She marched toward John and then reached past him to grab her towel.

"Hi hon," she said, forcing her voice to be casual. "I thought you'd be gone longer."

"Obviously," John growled.

Nina nearly winced. "How was the bike ride? Where are the kids?"

John took a step toward her, and Nina subconsciously took a step back. "The kids," said John slowly, "are in the camper. And thank goodness for that or they would have seen their own mother flagrantly disobeying the instructions I gave to them just days ago."

She stopped herself from falling backwards away from him and stood her ground. "I'm an adult, John. I know how to dive."

He leaned toward her, his eyes drilling into hers. "Let me be clear, Nina. No one is allowed to dive off that rock. If an Olympic gold medallist in diving were here right now, he or she would not be allowed to dive off that rock. Do you understand me?"

Nina nearly laughed, but the sound caught in her throat. "John, I..."

He stepped forward again and backed her into the fat trunk of a large tree. "What did I tell the kids I was going to do if they disobeyed me?"

She swallowed hard. "You said... you said you'd blister their... oh John, I'm sorry."

"You will be," he informed her, pinning her against the tree.

"What do you mean?" she began to get hysterical. She could feel his breath on her face. "What are you going to do? John? John?"

She didn't have long to wait. John grabbed her by the arm and dragged her a few feet into the woods.

She gasped loudly, and he leaned in close to her ear. "If you want an audience, you go ahead and make all the noise you want. I'll be happy to explain that I'm spanking my wife for breaking the rules of this campground."

When she heard those words, she began to cry. John placed his foot on a tree stump and flipped her over his strong thigh. He peeled off her bikini bottoms, still wet from the lake.

She struggled when she felt the air on her bare skin. John stopped her rebellion with a swift whack to her unclothed bottom. She lurched against his thigh as the pain swept through her. She bit her lip to keep from yelling. Silent tears ran down her cheeks.

She was still wet, and the swats seemed harsh against the moisture. Her bottom soon dried, though, as the heat increased.

John began to smack her hard now, whap after solid whap landing rapidly on reddening skin. She wiggled and cried, her tears falling faster now.

"What were you thinking?" John asked her, keeping up the pace of his smacks even as he spoke.

She couldn't answer. She could only shake her head furiously.

"You could have been seriously hurt, Nina." John seemed to use this fear to propel his arm faster. The slaps sounded to Nina like machine gun fire as they hit her bottom at a terribly quick pace.

Nina felt her legs begin to kick and her waist begin to twist. She was suspended in the air over John's thigh. He held her steadily against himself with one hand and punished her with the other.

"I cannot believe you," John said, finally slowing the spanks. Each one felt like a new assault on Nina's tender bottom.

"I'm sorry!" she wailed.

John lifted her up, and her hands flew behind her to rub her bottom furiously. She saw John hide a smirk, but she was too sore to care. Her bottom felt like it had been held over an open fire, like the hot dogs they'd cooked the evening before.

John watched her hop around for a moment or two. Then he said, "Turn around. Lemme see."

She eyed him suspiciously through her tears. "Why?"

John sighed and grabbed his small wife by one hand, turning her easily. He smacked her once on her blazing bottom.

"Yow!" Nina yelled.

"I want to see your bottom," John told her. "Hold still."

She did, feeling more than a little embarrassed at having John stare at her this way.

"It's red," John told her, "but no blisters."

She spun around to face him. "You weren't serious about blisters?"

He shook his head. "No. But I was very serious about the no swimming."

49

Nina sniffed. "You can't. I mean, I have to swim with the kids."

Her husband nodded. "I know that. But we're going to add a little bit to this punishment. You'll meet me here tomorrow morning for another spanking. I want your behind nice and sore for a couple of days at least."

Nina released the tears that she had managed to contain. "John, please don't do that."

He studied her grimly. "I had no idea you were capable of this level of disobedience. I need to make sure it ends right now."

"It ends, John. I promise," Nina said. She tugged at her bikini bottoms and winced as she pulled them up over her swollen bottom.

John folded his arms over his chest. "We'll come out here tomorrow morning before the kids wake up. And then we'll come once more the morning we leave."

Nina's mouth dropped open. "But I'll have to ride in the truck all day…"

"That's right," John told her. "And you will remember this lesson all the way home."

Nina sighed, but she knew that there would be no changing John's mind. She reminded herself that his integrity was something she loved about him.

"Let's go back and get the kids," said John. "They wanted to take you to lunch."

Nina groaned. "At the dock? With the wooden benches for seats?"

"That's right," John said. She could hear the amused undertone of his serious voice. Then he got firm. He looked into her eyes. "Young lady, if you ever…"

"I won't," Nina promised. "I won't ever."

"What would I do without you? What would the kids do without you?"

She sighed deeply. He was absolutely right. "It was stupid, John. I'm sorry."

He put an arm around her shoulder and led her out of the woods and back toward the camper. She felt her bottom burn and sting with every step. All she wanted to do was jump back into the cool lake.

But she had a lunch date with a wooden bench. And she had a family who loved her and needed her to stay alive and in one piece.

She took her husband's hand and walked toward her children.

Autumn Doubts

Her voice made Marnie's ears hurt.

"Well if it isn't Jackson Harrison," The high-pitched Southern drawl drifted toward Marnie and Jack as Heather made her way across the parking lot. She had her petite, manicured little hand in the air, and she was waving for all she was worth.

Marnie saw the dumb smile on her husband's face, and she groaned. Heather stepped between two cars in order to catch up to the couple. Marnie noticed that she was wearing her trademark denim shorts, cut off at the thigh. They made her legs look about eight feet long. Her tiny tummy peeked out from under a team t-shirt.

"Don't you just love these football games?" she said linking her arm through Jack's. She only glanced momentarily across him. "Hey Marne."

Marnie didn't return the greeting. She knew that Heather wouldn't notice. The three of them made their way into the crowd that poured toward the high school stadium. Here in the small town of Gladney, the Friday night football games were an area-wide event. They were especially important to Jack, who had once been the team's quarterback. Marnie knew that he liked to relive his days on the field, watching the new stars do their thing. High school had been a good time for him, and Marnie tried hard to remember that.

She herself had spent most of the high school football games working the concession stands with the rest of the debate team. Marnie had been a geek in high school, and there was no getting around it. Not only a debate champion, she was also on the academic team. She had even lettered in chess. Plump and uncoordinated since childhood, Marnie had taken social dance to fulfill her physical education requirement. She was careful to make sure that she never broke a sweat, but she could still do a mean foxtrot.

Marnie and Jack never knew each other in school. The towns in the area were small, but the school district was a consolidation of the rural kids from miles around. Jack and Marnie didn't grow up near each other, and they didn't run in the same circles.

In fact, they never met until college. They were both active in the campus Christian ministry, and they ended up in a Bible study group together. By that time, Jack had lost some of his jock attitude from school. And Marnie had blossomed, as her mother would say. She was still a little bit overweight, but contact lenses had replaced the bulky glasses and she had finally figured out what to do with her unruly hair. Jack was attracted to her instantly. Marnie couldn't believe that it was physical, and she had always thought that it was mostly that he respected her faith and intelligence. For her part, she enjoyed everything about the crazy, athletic boy. He was given to random, spontaneous acts that left Marnie breathless. They truly enjoyed each other's company. Over time, this friendship grew into love. They were married soon after college graduation. They moved back to Gladney so that Jack could go into business with his father.

They had both been shocked to discover that they'd gone to the same high school. Jack had graduated just two years ahead of Marnie and even ran track with her older brother. Once they'd talked about it, they eventually discovered that they had several connections. They had just never met.

Heather Taylor was one of those connections. She was easily the most popular girl in Marnie's class. The Homecoming queen was revered for her beautiful body, silky long hair and pretty face. Even Marnie had to admit that she was stunning. Marnie's brother had been in love with her, along with most of the boys in school.

Worst of all, she had dated Jack.

Marnie looked at her now and sighed to see that she hadn't changed a bit. It had been five years since their graduation, and she was still beautiful. She was trim and toned in all the right places. Men couldn't seem to help staring at her.

Marnie felt like a cow.

She knew she wasn't hideous. She had even been called pretty a time or two. But she'd never been slender, and she'd gained some weight after getting married. Then she gained some more while she was pregnant with JJ, the five-month-old angel who was staying with her mother that night. A new mom, she often felt tired and rundown.

Next to fresh-faced Heather, she knew she must seem like the walking dead.

"How is that gorgeous baby?" Heather asked them, although she seemed to be addressing her question to Jack.

"He's wonderful," Jack told her, not loosening his grip on Marnie's hand. "Let's grab those seats near the fifty. You coming, Heather?"

"Of course!" Heather replied with enthusiasm.

Marnie groaned so loudly that Jack turned to look at her.

"You okay, Marne?" he asked, those blue eyes full of concern.

She tossed a fake smile at her husband and allowed her eyes to narrow. "Just fine," she said. "We're gonna sit with Heather!"

Oblivious, Heather skipped ahead to hold their seats.

Jack leaned down toward Marnie. "What is wrong with you?" he whispered.

"You know I don't like her," Marnie whispered back.

"Don't be ridiculous," he told her. "She's a nice girl."

Marnie rolled her eyes, and Jack sighed. She hated fighting with him. But even more than that, she hated that he still seemed to want to be friends with that awful woman. Sometimes when she let herself think too much about it, her imagination led her to a dark place where she found herself wondering if Jack wanted to be with Heather. She wondered if he looked at Marnie with her sagging tummy and ratty hair and wished that he'd married Heather all those years ago.

Marnie shook her head to unlock the image. She sat next to Jack, who sat next to Heather.

Heather flipped her long hair over one shoulder and then made flirtatious eyes at Jack. Marnie felt a little bit sick and had to look away.

When Marnie had first asked Jack about the relationship, he told her that he and Heather had just been a high school fling. He said he'd only dated her because it seemed like the football quarterback was supposed to take out the homecoming queen. He knew after a few weeks that it wasn't going anywhere. He said that they'd ended things because Heather had wanted them to sleep together. He was already a religious guy by then, and he wasn't willing.

At the time, Marnie had believed him. But now face to face with Heather, she had to wonder if that was what had really happened between them.

"I need something to drink," Heather said suddenly. "You want a diet soda, Marnie?"

Marnie bristled at Heather's insinuation that she needed to drink diet soda. "I'll take a lemonade," she said frostily.

"Sure thing," Heather replied smoothly. "Jackson, sugar, could you help me with the drinks? I don't think I can carry them all myself. Marnie can hold down the fort. Can't you, Marne?"

Jack squeezed Marnie's hand and stood up. "I'll be right back."

She nodded and watched them step over several people to get to the walkway. Once there, Heather slipped her tiny arm into Jack's.

Marnie swallowed hard. She couldn't take her eyes off them. She saw them standing in line at the concession stand. He laughed at something she said. Then Heather leaned in close and whispered something into Jack's ear. Marnie shivered.

By the time Heather and Jack returned, Marnie's insides felt like ice. She glared at her husband as he handed her the lemonade.

"Your husband is so funny!" Heather said gleefully. "He tells the silliest stories."

Marnie pursed her lips. "Oh yeah?"

"Why yes," Heather said. "But we have some funny stories of our own. Don't we Jackson? Remember that time we went down to that restaurant by the dock? Have you been there Marnie?"

Marnie shook her head, but didn't trust herself to speak.

Jack said, "We haven't been out much since the baby was born."

Heather shook her head in disapproval. "Marnie, you mighta just had a baby but it's time for you to get back out there with your man. Take off that baby weight and get yourself into something pretty. You need to hold that boy just in case someone else tries to steal him away."

The glint in Heather's eye was unmistakable. A wave of hot anger shot through Marnie's chest. She stood. And then she dumped her lemonade right on Heather's bleach blonde head.

Heather shrieked. The people in the rows behind them began to laugh. Heads turned to look. Jack jumped up and grabbed Marnie by the arm. He pulled her out of the stands and then back behind the bleachers. Marnie had to hop to keep up with his long strides.

"What are you doing?" His face was incredulous, his eyes confused.

"She wants you, Jack! Surely you can see that!" Marnie spat. "Or maybe you like the attention, and you just don't care!"

Jack crossed his arms over his chest. He was a large man with broad shoulders and a big frame. "What are you talking about?"

"She's been hot for you since high school. Come on, you're not stupid." Marnie glared at him.

"Neither are you," Jack told her bluntly. "Look, I don't care what Heather wants. I am married to you. You are the mother of my child. Or have you forgotten?"

"The question is, have you forgotten?" Marnie said, returning fire.

The couple stood looking hard at each other as several moments passed. They heard the sounds of the football game behind them. The band began to play.

Finally, Jack spoke. "This is not right."

"That's what I've been trying to tell you!" Marnie said passionately. "She's throwing herself at you!"

"I am talking about you, Marnie. I am talking about you and me." Jackson held her by the shoulders. "Where is this insecurity coming from?"

Marnie's eyes began to fill with liquid. "I'm not insecure."

"Girl, you are more insecure than a skyscraper built on quicksand," Jack said. He straightened his baseball cap.

"It's Heather!" Marnie insisted.

"It's you," Jack said quietly. "And we're gonna fix this."

He took her by the hand and led her toward the school.

She followed cautiously. "Where are we going?"

"Pumpkin sale," said Jack.

"What?" She tried to pull away, but her husband had a tight grip on her hand. He dragged her along, and she stumbled to keep up.

Soon she saw where he was headed. On the other side of the high school some club or another had set up hay bales and pumpkins for a sale the next day. She looked down toward the stadium where the lights continued to blaze. The crowd was faint, but she could still hear them yelling.

"What? What are we doing here?" she asked, sounding more annoyed than she was.

"We are gonna talk," said Jack. "Sit down."

She seated herself on the hay bale he offered. He straddled it with his long legs and eased himself down beside her.

"First off, I am offended that you would think that I would have any kind of interest in Heather or in any other woman," Jack told her.

Marnie rolled her eyes.

"Marnie," Jack snapped. "You believe that?"

"I don't know," Marnie said. It came out like a pout. The truth was that she didn't really believe he would look at someone else, not really. But she was angry and hurt. She wanted to hurt him too.

Jack sighed. "Well then," he said. He flipped one long leg back over the hay. Then he pulled Marnie down over his lap.

"Jack, quit it! Jack!" Marnie protested.

He twisted her easily so that her denim-skirted rump was over his knees. Then he smacked her hard on the fanny.

She yelled, and he smacked her again. The force was strong, and the impact stung.

"I love you!" he told her, whacking away with every word. "I don't love Heather or anybody else. Just you!"

The pain in her bottom was beginning to increase. She squeezed her eyes shut and whined.

"Am I getting through to you?" he asked her, adding several more hard thwacks to her thighs. His hand made contact with some bare skin, and she yelped.

"Do you have something to say?" he asked her.

"I..." she began. Her bottom hurt. "Can I get up?"

"No," he said.

She sighed loudly, and he swatted her again. "Fine. Jack, I know you love me. I'm not saying you don't love me. But... let's face it. I don't look like Heather. I never did. You love me for my brains and my sense of humor. But Jack, I never looked like that! How can I compete with that?"

The last words came out in a rush, and Marnie started to cry. Jack sucked in air.

"Marnie Harrison," he began. His voice sounded threatening, and Marnie felt herself tense. "You honestly believe I am not attracted to you?"

"I... I know you are... to my mind, but..." she stammered.

He rested a heavy hand on her bottom. "This is partly my fault," he said.

"What? Jack, can I get up?"

57

"No," he swatted her again. "I guess I haven't made it clear how I feel about you."

"I don't need you to tell me a bunch of lies," Marnie said softly. "It's okay. I know I'm not beautiful."

"Not beautiful?" Jack repeated. "What…"

He didn't finish the sentence. Instead he flipped her skirt up to her waist. She was shocked to find herself displaying her ample panty covered bottom to anyone who happened to wander by the high school.

"Jack!" she yelled.

He answered with a stinging smack to her right bottom cheek and then matched it with one to her left. "It is true that I love your brains," he said. "Although you haven't been showing too much of them lately."

He swatted her again, and she jumped.

"But for you to say you're not beautiful…" he shook his head and then he smacked her hard.

"Ouch!" she cried.

He did it again. "You have always been beautiful! I have always, always been attracted to you!"

His hand landed again and again on the panties. She bucked, kicking her feet up into the air.

"I love everything about you, Marnie. I love your eyes. I love your hair. I love your little earlobes."

He spanked her hard now, alternating cheeks.

Marnie was stunned, tears rolling down her nose.

"And I cannot get enough of this behind," he told her, adding several hard smacks for emphasis.

She wasn't sure anymore if her tears came from the pain in her bottom or the pain in her heart. She shuddered.

"I don't want a woman like Heather. For goodness sake, Marne. Give me some credit!" With this, he tugged her panties down to her knees.

Marnie panicked. She began to squirm and kick. She was terrified that someone would see her like this, would witness her husband spanking her naked, overweight backside. The thought of it made her crazy.

Jack did not share her concern. He peppered her bare bottom with hot smacks. "You take my breath away every time I look at you," he told her. He brought his hand down hard in the center of her bottom. "How do you not see that?"

She went limp over his knees, his words sinking into her head. "I don't know," she whimpered. "I don't know. I just feel so unattractive."

He lifted her up and gathered her into his arms. "Baby, you should never feel that way. I always want you."

Her hot, bare bottom sank onto his jeans as she settled herself against his chest. He breathed onto her neck.

"I always want you," he repeated.

"Jack," she whispered.

That was all it took. He flopped down behind the wall of hay, taking her with him. She fell beside him onto the ground. Her sore bottom landed on some loose hay, and she squealed in pain.

Jack rolled toward her. "Honey, I love you too much to let you put this marriage in danger. If you ever, ever talk like that again I will spank your behind until you can't sit down for a week. You understand me?"

She did. She understood him completely now. She nodded and kissed him hard on the mouth.

He answered with a breathy sigh, and then he rolled her back into the hay.

The "Camping" Stories

Grown-Ups

Katie sat on the picnic table and grinned at her husband. Rick was perfection in Katie's newly married eyes. His broad shoulders and muscular arms created a perfect respite for her at night, and she thought that she could stare into his beautiful eyes forever. She laughed to herself. The rest of him wasn't bad either.

He was standing a few feet away from her talking to a group of men. He shot her a secret smile, and she flashed him a grin. She lifted herself up off the table and made her way toward him.

"Do you have a good group?" she asked him.

He grinned. "I think so," he said. "We're trying to split up the wild ones so that no one has too much to handle."

"I'm glad I have girls," Katie told him. She stared into the bright sunshine. Woodlands Youth Camp had been one of Katie's favorite places since she'd first arrived as a camper at the age of ten. She'd camped every summer since then and had become a counselor-in-training and then a full-fledged counselor as soon as she was old enough. When she and Rick had first started dating, she'd talked him into being a counselor too. This was their first summer at Woodlands as a married couple. She knew that they'd be spending many wonderful times here in the future. She hoped that one day their own children would come here as campers.

Most of the female counselors were inside the large dining hall, but Katie had chosen to stay with her husband. The only trouble with camp was that they had to be away from each other for most of the week. Even married counselors were discouraged from public displays of affection. No one wanted to set a bad example for impressionable teenage campers.

"They're here!" Katie called. She turned toward the dining hall. "They're here!"

The other female counselors spilled from the doors of the large building as two school buses rumbled up onto the gravel driveway. As soon as the doors of the buses opened, kids began to pour out.

The Camp Director, Eve, began directing children to their counselors.

Katie had five girls in her cabin between the ages of twelve and fourteen. She knew them all from her time as a Youth Group volunteer.

Emma Campbell arrived first. The youngest of the group, Emma was soft spoken and sweet. She smiled shyly when Katie said hello. Emma was followed by Charli and Briana, inseparable best friends. They had originally been assigned to different cabins but had begged to be allowed to stay together. It was Katie who had given into their pleas. Both children were giggly examples of young teenage girlhood. Briana was of African descent with dark, shining skin and eyes. Charli was as pale as a ghost and had baby blue eyes and light blonde hair. Katie had spoken to Charli's mother just that morning when she had called to remind Katie to make sure Charli always wore sunscreen and a hat. Katie noticed that Charli's hat was sticking out of her duffle bag rather than being worn. Katie pulled it out and plopped it on her head.

"My hair!" Charli said.

Katie grinned. "It's camp. No one cares about your hair."

"I do," Charli mumbled, but she kept the hat in place.

Nina and Sophie were the last two girls to arrive. Sophie was known as bookish and intelligent, while Nina was the kind of girl who always expected to be the star of the show. No one really knew why they were friends, but they got along very well.

Girls who were known not to get along had been put into different groups. Katie was happy to hear that. Although some counselors had argued that it was good for children to learn to get along with everyone, she felt that it was better to avoid conflict if possible.

She rounded up her group and marched them toward their cabin. She waved as she passed Rick, who was still putting his group of boys together.

"See you at lunch!" she called. He winked at her flirtatiously and she smiled. Her man was the best.

She and Rick had managed to finagle their way into having their groups seated together during meals. Katie was glad because those were going to be among the only times she would spend with Rick during the coming week. She knew she would miss him.

The campers were excited and boisterous as they chose their bunks and put their things away. Even shy Emma seemed enthusiastic, and Katie was glad.

Katie fell onto her bunk in the front of the cabin and waited until they had settled down.

"What should we do this afternoon?" she asked them.

"Swimming!" Charli, Briana and Nina shouted together.

Katie had to wait for their giggles and shrieks to subside before she answered them. "We can't go swimming until tomorrow. The lifeguard doesn't arrive until then."

"We don't need a lifeguard," Nina said. "We all know how to swim."

All five girls nodded and looked at her hopefully.

"You can all swim?"

Five heads nodded together.

"I'm a Level 5 swimmer," said Briana. "And so is Charli."

"That's almost Junior Lifeguard," Charli said.

Katie nodded. "And you other girls can swim?"

Emma, Nina and Sophie bobbed their heads enthusiastically.

Katie thought it through. It wasn't as if the girls were non-swimmers. And she herself had taken swim lessons all the way through the Junior Lifeguard Level. But she was pretty sure that the Camp Director had signed something with the insurance company that said they would always use a lifeguard. "It's a camp rule, guys," she said finally. "I don't think I can bend it."

"No one else will be out there," Nina reminded her. "Why do they have to know?"

Katie considered this. It was true that most likely no one would even ask.

"You could be our lifeguard," Emma suggested.

"Yeah!" said Charli, and Emma beamed with pride that she had made a good suggestion.

The girls were just too persuasive. She gave in. "Okay," she said. "We'll swim after lunch, but just for an hour."

The girls cheered. "You're the best!" said Sophie. Katie felt terrific. It was worth it to her to bend some rules if it meant that the girls would like her so much.

They were a few minutes late for lunch, and Rick's group was already seated by the time they arrived. The girls moved quickly through the buffet line and took their seats.

"How's it going?" Rick asked his wife with a smile as she took her place across from him.

"Going great!" she answered. She nodded at the boys, who looked sweet all lined up at the table. "How your group?"

"Can't complain," Rick answered.

Everyone sat quietly as the Camp Director gave a little speech. Then they all dug into their lunch. The dining hall was alive with the sounds of eating. Forks clanked against metal dishes and children shouted and laughed.

Katie was absently talking to Rick when she saw a piece of cooked carrot fly across the table and smack one of Rick's kids in the head.

"Hey!" yelled Troy, the injured party. He was a twelve-year-old with curly hair and a sweet smile. Katie knew that her girls all thought he was adorable.

Katie was certain that the carrot came from Nina, but she pretended not to notice.

Troy picked up a spoonful of mashed potatoes and aimed it across the table.

"Put it down," said Rick calmly but forcefully.

Troy obeyed but looked wounded. "But Nina did it first!"

"I am not responsible for Nina's behavior," Rick said, looking pointedly at his wife.

Katie glanced down the table at her row of angelic girls. "I'm sure it was an accident," she said. All of her girls nodded.

"Uh huh," Rick murmured.

Before too long, another carrot flew.

"Stop it!" Troy shouted.

Rick looked at Katie who shrugged her shoulders and smiled at him. "That's enough, girls," she said in a sing-song voice.

A few minutes later, a forkful of baked beans made its way into another boy's hair.

Evan looked at his counselor. "Can I please throw my hot dog at her?"

Rick shook his head. "No," he said. He looked at his wife. "Katie? Are you going to do something about this?"

"Girls," Katie sang happily. "Eat your lunches please."

Rick sighed and moved his steely gaze from Katie to Nina. "Nina Harper," he said sternly. "If one more piece of food gets thrown across this table, you and I are going outside for a private talk."

Nina blushed, embarrassed to have been reprimanded in front of the boys. Katie grew furious.

"Can I talk to you, please?" she said to her husband. She nodded to the corner of the dining hall. "Over there?"

"I'd like that very much," Rick snapped, placing his napkin on the table. He looked at the boys and then the girls. "We'll be right over there," he reminded them.

Rick followed Katie to the corner of the dining hall. As soon as they were out of earshot, she spun on him.

"Don't discipline my girls," she said.

"Someone has to," Rick told her. "You're letting Nina behave like a brat."

"I have my own style with them," Katie told him.

"Your style needs some backbone," Rick countered. "Kids need boundaries."

"Kids need freedom, too!" Katie answered. "Besides, I want to be their friend. I don't want to be some authority figure."

"You are an authority figure," Rick told her. He looked at his watch. "Lunch is almost over. Are you going hiking this afternoon? We could talk then."

Katie sighed. "Um… actually, I told them we could go swimming in the lake."

Rick raised his eyebrows. "You know there's no lifeguard."

"It's just for an hour," she explained.

"Katie!" Rick shook his head. "You could get this camp in serious trouble."

"It's not a big deal," she said.

Rick pulled her in close and looked her square in the eye. "No swimming," he said. "Do we understand each other?"

She fought the urge to roll her eyes and twisted her mouth instead. "I understand."

He took her forearm. "I mean it, Katie."

"No swimming," she said. "I hear you."

He gave her a quick kiss. "We'll talk about this later."

She watched him return to her boys.

The girls were upset about not being able to swim, but Katie told them that it just wasn't possible. They were smart girls, and they knew Rick had something to do with it.

"Well, he's right," Katie told them as they sat on their bunks. "It is a camp rule."

"We should do something to get him back," Charli suggested.

"Yeah!" Briana agreed.

Katie shook her head. "I don't think so."

"Come on, Katie," said Nina, whose pride was still wounded. "It'll just be a prank."

She laughed. Pranks were a perfectly normal part of camp life. "What did you have in mind?" she asked.

The girls thought it over. "Honey in their socks?" said Briana.

"Peanut butter in their shoes?" Nina put in.

Katie smiled. "That sounds great!"

Sophie took over. Everyone turned to look at the pixie-haired girl with the glasses on her nose. "We can get the supplies at dinner. We'll have to go at night. You know they leave their shoes on the cabin steps in case they have to go to the bathroom."

Katie laughed, imagining her husband with his feet covered in peanut butter. It was a classic camp prank, one she'd pulled herself as a camper. She remembered sneaking past her counselor in the middle of the night, and she also remembered how angry her counselor had been when she found out what they'd done. She smiled because her girls wouldn't have to sneak anywhere. Their counselor would be right with them. She was the coolest counselor in the history of Woodlands.

The whole cabin was in a terrific mood through dinner and evening campfire. When it was finally bedtime, they were ready to put the plan in motion.

"Let's give them some time to fall asleep," said Sophie. "Katie, do you think Rick lets them stay up past light's out?"

Katie shook her head. "No way. Rick's a rule-follower."

"Great!" said Sophie. " Emma, do you have the peanut butter?"

Emma held it up.

Nina broke in. "Bri's got the honey!"

Briana grinned and nodded.

"We're ready," said Katie.

About an hour later, they snuck across the campground. Katie had warned them to be as quiet as possible since being out for any reason other than to go to the bathroom was breaking a major camp rule. Girls being in the boys' part of the campground after lights out was an even more serious rule. They would all be in big trouble if they were caught.

Katie's job was to act as a lookout. She watched while Emma, the smallest and quietest of the group, snuck up to the boys' cabin. She carefully filled each shoe with honey, while the other girls snickered.

Briana and Charli followed with the peanut butter.

They were almost finished when Katie heard something in the woods behind her. She froze. Was it a wild animal? There were bears in this area. She turned around to look and then cried out. A large hand closed over her mouth, and an arm prevented her from struggling. At first she had the crazy thought she was being abducted, but then she heard a familiar voice.

"Kathryn, you are in big trouble."

It was Rick, and he was livid.

All five girls had turned away from their mission and were staring at Rick and Katie.

Rick let her go and then regarded the delinquents. He spoke in an angry whisper. "Get back to the cabin, now."

The girls shuffled away. Rick looked at Katie. "Go ahead. We're right behind you."

The little group made its way back to the girls' cabin. Rick delivered a stinging lecture and promised them kitchen duty instead of swimming for the next two afternoons. "I don't want to catch any of you out of these beds until daylight," he told them. "Katie will be back in a few minutes."

Then he grabbed his wife by the arm and dragged her out of the cabin.

"Rick," she whispered furiously. "Where are you taking me?"

He walked fast, and she had to hop along behind him to keep up. When they reached the dining hall, he unlocked the door and pushed her inside.

"What were you thinking?" he demanded, his six-foot frame towering over her.

"It was a prank, Rick! All campers play pranks!" she said nervously.

"Campers play pranks," he told her evenly. "You are a counselor. Your job is to discourage pranks, not to lead them."

"I want to be their friend," she whined. "I want them to like me."

He shook his head and sighed deeply. "Honey, you are an adult. If kids like you all of the time, then you are not doing your job. What's going to happen when we have children? Am I going to always be the bad guy?"

She shrugged. "I don't know. Can't we both be good guys?"

"I will not allow this to become a theme in our relationship, Katie." He reached around her and took a wooden serving spoon off the buffet table. "From now on when you act like a child, you'll get treated like one."

Her blue eyes got wide and she began to back away. "They're going to need that spoon tomorrow."

"I'm sure they have others," he said, staying less then a foot away from her.

He finally backed her into a table. She leaned away from him. "Rick... please. I'll do better."

"Turn around," he said. "And take down your shorts."

"My shorts!" she repeated. "I can't be naked in the dining hall!"

He actually chuckled. "This is what it's like when you act like a little girl. Now get those shorts off, or I'll do it for you."

Katie undid the zipper on her shorts, watching her husband with pleading eyes. When they were undone, he reached over and pushed them down over her hips.

She stood in the dining hall with just her white cotton panties covering her lower half.

He looked at her for a long minute. "Katie, what do you think I would do if one of those girls was our daughter?"

Katie swallowed. She knew her husband's feelings about the discipline of children. "You'd spank her."

"That's right," he said. "And what makes you think you should be treated any differently when you pull a childish stunt?"

She shook her head. She didn't have an answer for him. "I don't know, Rick."

"Turn around," he said. "Put your hands on the table, and don't take them off."

She did as she was told. Rick stepped to her left side and put an arm around her waist. Then he began to paddle her panties with the spoon.

He was spanking her hard, and it hurt immediately. She began to kick her legs and wiggle back and forth. Rick held her tight, and she found that she couldn't go very far. In frustration and embarrassment, she began to cry.

The spoon moved swiftly, landing on each part of Katie's bottom. The pain was harsh, and she began to cry. She tried not to make too much noise, but she soon found that she was no longer in control of herself. Her bottom hurt, and she felt ashamed of herself.

After several minutes, Rick stopped spanking her and waited for her tears to calm. Then he spoke.

"Katie, why do you think there are rules about the kids being out at night?"

Katie bit her lower lip. She hadn't considered that. "I don't know," she admitted.

"There are places and animals in this campground that are dangerous in the dark," he told her. "There are lots of ways for kids to get hurt at night."

She realized she knew this, but somehow it hadn't mattered that evening. "I guess I wasn't thinking."

"I can see that," Rick growled. "And what about encouraging vandalism?"

"I didn't…" she began.

"You think any of us is ever going to get the peanut butter out of our shoes?"

She remembered, too late, that she'd had to pay for a new pair of sneakers the year she and her friends had pulled that trick. "I forgot," she said quietly.

"That's because you were thinking like a child, Katie," Rick told her bluntly. "It's unacceptable, honey. You are not a child, and you have a responsibility to these kids."

Katie began to cry again. "I just wanted them to like me!"

In one quick motion, Rick pulled Katie's panties to her knees. "Rick!" she cried.

"How did that work for you, Kate? The kids like you, but you're standing in the dining hall with a bare, pink bottom that's about to be red. Is it worth that?"

She shook her head wildly. "No!"

"Remember this," he instructed her. With his large hand, he spanked her already tender skin. She wailed and struggled, but he held her tight.

"From now on you're going to act like a grown-up," he told her as he swatted her bottom, flattening one cheek and then the other.

"You're going to think like an adult, and you're going to be a good role model for these girls."

Her tears flowed like someone had turned on a faucet. "I'm sorry!" she said. "Please, Rick. I'm sorry."

He gave her ten more swats for good measure before he let her go. She looked up at him, her face sad and repentant.

"You can pull your pants up," he told her.

She did. It wasn't comfortable to feel the fabric over her punished bottom, but it was better than being exposed.

"First thing tomorrow we're going to see Eve," he told her. "You're going tell her what you did and apologize."

She sniffed. "Okay."

"And you're going to tell her you got your tail spanked for it," Rick added.

Katie cried harder, but she agreed. "Okay."

"We'll have to call the kids' parents. The boys are going to need new shoes, and the girls' folks are going to have to pay for them."

She groaned. She hadn't thought of that either.

"And I'm going to make sure that the girls' parents have some alone time with them in Eve's office in case they'd like to have a discussion about personal responsibility," said Rick. "You'll be apologizing to them, too.

She nodded and hung her head. "I'm sorry, Rick. I really am. I'm going to try to be an adult from now on."

Rick lifted her chin so that she was looking into his eyes. "I love you. I even love your childishness and your irresponsibility. We just have to make sure they only come out when it's appropriate. I'm going to help you do that, okay?"

She leaned against his chest and nodded her head. And for the millionth time since she'd known him, she silently thanked heaven for bringing Rick into her life.

The Retreat

Charity's shoes kept falling off.

"Not again!" she wailed. She bent her leg so that she could grab the heel of her off-white sandals.

Tom looked up from the breakfast table where he was reading a newspaper. "They're too big. I told you not to buy them."

She sneered at him. "Well, they're cute!"

Tom shrugged and went back to his paper.

Charity flung her giant, purple duffle bag onto the kitchen table. Tom had to move his cereal out of the way to keep it from being hit. "Are you even packed?" she demanded.

Her husband sighed. He didn't want to go away on this overnight trip. He wanted to go to the baseball game with his buddies. They'd had tickets for weeks. "Not yet."

"Then get packed!" Charity demanded. "Honestly, Tom. Can't you do anything without me telling you?"

Tom got up from the table and looked at his wife. "Where are we going again?"

Charity put some bug spray into her overnight bag. "It's a marriage retreat. There are two spots open, and Lynne really wants us to go."

Tom noted that Charity had never once asked whether he wanted to go. She'd simply told Lynne that they would be there.

Charity looked at her husband standing there watching her. "Go get packed!" she said, waving him from the kitchen. "Go on!"

Tom turned and climbed the stairs to their bedroom.

The retreat was being held at a lovely park an hour or so outside of the city. It was spring, and the trees had begun to be filled in with leaves. The azaleas were in bloom, and daffodils lined the walkways.

Charity moved along like a buffalo in a dust storm. She held her head down as if she were pushing against something as she made her way along the narrow path. Tom straggled two feet behind her.

Inside the main building, people were walking around everywhere. There were several tables set up for registration. Charity marched to the longest table and signed them both in.

"Men on the left and women on the right," said the older woman in charge of registrations. She handed Charity two name tags.

Charity was surprised. "You mean we won't be together?"

"There are two separate areas," the woman told her. "Men on the left and women on the right."

Charity rearranged the bag on her shoulder and turned around to look for Tom. He was standing in the doorway. When she got back to him, she handed him a name tag. "You're on the left."

He took the small tag and held it in his hand. "Left of what?"

"I dunno," she admitted. "Follow the other guys, I guess."

He pushed his glasses up the bridge of his nose. "I guess I'll see you later."

She watched him lumber off to join a group of men across the room. She sighed to see how helpless he looked without her. She thought that she should go over to the group and get him started, but she saw that she would be the only woman there. She hoped he remembered to pack enough supplies. She thought for the fourth or fifth time that she should have supervised his packing instead of simply checking his bag when he was finished. She made a mental note to do it herself the next time.

She put a hand to her blonde curls and looked for the women. They were standing together in a group of around twenty. She peered at the group until she found Lynne.

"I'm so glad you could come," her friend greeted her when she approached. Lynne was a petite woman with straight dark hair and relaxed brown eyes. She was a mother of four, but she never looked frazzled or concerned. In fact, there was always a calmness about Lynne that Charity admired and envied. Charity had met her at the gym, and soon after that Lynne invited her to their church. Charity and

Tom had attended services ever since. "Girls, this is my good friend Charity."

Charity had met some of the women before, but she didn't remember any of their names. She greeted them and spoke casually until it was time to move onto the day's activities.

Most of the morning was spent getting everyone settled into cabins. Charity was surprised to learn that the couples wouldn't be staying together. In fact, it seemed that they would hardly be spending any time together at all. She wondered how Tom was doing in his group. She worried about him socially, thinking of him as someone not quite capable of taking care of himself. She hoped Lynne's husband, Joe, would take responsibility for him.

Over in the men's area, Tom was the life of the party.

The men were all trying to catch their breath after Tom's crazy tale of going fishing with his friends.

"You all ended up in the lake?" Joe laughed.

"And all the fish did, too," Tom put in. "We came back soaked to the skin, and we had nothing for dinner."

Joe tossed his bag onto one of the beds. "I've never seen you talk so much."

"I don't usually have a chance," Tom muttered.

"What was that?"

Tom shook his head. "Nothing. What's on the agenda?"

That afternoon the men gathered in the large conference room for a discussion on marriage. It was a cavernous, mostly empty room with wooden walls and floors. The men sat in folding chairs in a disorganized semi-circle, leaving a small space in the center. Joe stood in front of the group and addressed his friends. The open space caused an echo when he spoke.

"We're lucky today, guys. We've got Frank Morris here to talk to us about our wives. You might have heard of him. He's written several books on male authoritative marriage and parenting. Make him feel welcome."

The men clapped as an older gentleman stepped into the center of the room. He took a chair and sat down. "I'm not really here to make a speech," he said. "I'd like to have some discussion instead. We can all learn from each other."

He looked around the room and took everyone in with his gaze. "We're all married men here, and that means we've got some things in common. Women are wonderful, and we all know that. But all marriages have conflict. What are some of the conflicts in yours?"

One man spoke up. "Parenting. My wife thinks I'm too strict with the kids. I think she lets them get away with murder."

Another man said, "We don't agree on how to spend money."

Someone else said, "Sex. Can I say that? I'm a little more... enthusiastic than she is."

There were chuckles all around.

Tom wanted to speak up. He wanted to say that everything was wrong with his marriage. He loved Charity. He loved her so much that sometimes it hurt. But he felt like he had no presence in their relationship. He felt like an accessory in her wardrobe. He wanted to say all this, but he kept quiet. Tom was not one to be free with his feelings.

"These are all good topics," said Frank. "Now let's talk about a traditional marriage. In a traditional marriage, we're the head of the household. Now that's a huge responsibility on us, and sometimes we're really going to feel it."

The men nodded in agreement.

"We expect our wives to be submissive," Frank continued. "But what exactly does that mean? Does it mean that her opinion isn't valued? Does it mean that we control her? Of course not. We are supposed to treasure our wives. We are to treat them like they are the most precious thing on earth. We're to protect and nurture them, and we are always to keep their best interests in mind."

Tom looked around. Most of the men seemed to understand exactly what Frank was saying. He was a little lost.

Frank went on. "We owe it to our wives to be the leaders of our households. It's our job to always be thinking about what it best for them, and for the kids. We've got to be trustworthy so that she can place her faith in us."

Joe leaned forward, his elbows resting on his knees. "That's my philosophy. When I make a decision for my family, I always ask myself if it's the best thing for Lynne and the kids. If it is, then I go ahead with it. Sometimes Lynne disagrees, but she respects my choices and my place as the head of our relationship."

"That's the way it's done," said Frank.

Tom wanted some answers. He addressed the group. "But what if you can't lead? What if you've lost control over your relationship?"

A couple of the men actually nodded, looking curiously at Frank.

The speaker grew serious. "That's a common problem," he said. "All too often in our society, women are taking charge. That's just not the way a traditionalist believe it was intended it to be. It's not fair to us, it's not fair to our kids and it's ultimately not fair to our wives."

Tom wrinkled his forehead. "But how do you stop it? My wife is a powerhouse. I hate to admit it, but she steamrolls me."

"What are you doing about it?" Frank asked him honestly. "How do you react?"

Tom sighed. "I walk away," he admitted. "I ignore it."

"That's a common mistake," said Frank. "The problem with that response is that it just makes the problem worse. It makes her think that you want her to be in charge."

"And it gives her a terrible sense of insecurity," Joe put in. "Lynne and I had this problem early in our marriage."

Tom was struck dumb. It had never once occurred to him that he was encouraging Charity when he ignored her behavior.

"You've got to act," Frank said. "You've got to step up and be the leader in your marriage."

Tom considered this.

Meanwhile, the women were outside in an open field. The air was cool and clean, and they lounged on large blankets in the grass.

"We didn't get a speaker like the boys did," Lynne explained. "But we can still talk about marriage. Anything going on with you?"

Some of the women brought up small problems. One talked about her children and another about the stresses of buying a new house. One woman discussed how she and her husband were trying to decide if she should work outside the home.

A young wife, Julie, spoke up from the back. "I did something crazy last week. I spent a ton of money on a new outfit. I don't know why I did it. I was just feeling stressed out, and I was looking for a way to get calm. Jack wasn't happy."

Lynne nodded. "What happened?"

"We got into a big fight," Julie said. "I said some pretty awful things. And then he spanked me."

Charity looked up in alarm. Lynne didn't seem the least bit surprised.

"How did it end?" she asked.

"I was able to realize that spending money is not the way to make myself feel better," Julie said. "And I remembered that Jack is my leader. I have to be obedient to him."

Charity was flabbergasted. She had never heard someone speak this way about marriage. "Your husband spanks you?" she asked.

Julie nodded. "Yes. It's a decision we made when we got married. It's part of my submission to him as head of the household."

Charity looked at Lynne, who smiled. "I know it can seem strange if you're new to the lifestyle, but this kind of relationship works in many traditional homes. It helps us to remember to be submissive to our husbands."

Charity was amazed. She had never considered such a thing. "But why do you want to be submissive?" she asked. She hoped she didn't sound judgmental, but she was curious.

Some of the women laughed.

Lynne smiled kindly. "Most of us asked that same question at some point in our lives. We believe in a structure of marriage such that the man is the head of the household, and the woman is his submissive partner."

"Besides," Julie said, "it makes life a whole lot easier when you don't have to be responsible for every little thing. I like following my husband's lead. It makes me feel free to pursue my passions and to be myself. I know he'll take care of me, and I don't have to worry."

Charity nodded. She had no idea what it would be like to feel that kind of freedom and security. What would life be like if Tom took charge? She smiled to herself. She could not imagine Tom leading anything. "But what if your husband isn't the leader type?" she asked. "What if he just sits there and waits for you to tell him what to do?"

Lynne laughed. "Maybe you should just sit there and wait him out."

Another woman nodded. Her name was Emily. "My husband was like that once. We were about to get divorced, and I didn't know what to do. I just announced to him one day that I wouldn't be making any more decisions. I told him that he should let me know if he needed me to do something. It took a lot of patience on my part, but he finally came around. Our relationship has never been better."

"It's good for the children, too," said a middle-aged woman who sat next to Charity. "It's better for kids to see their father as a strong, authoritative figure."

Charity pursed her lips sadly. "We never had children," she admitted. "It was because I didn't think I could run the house and my marriage and still have any energy left over for any children. Tom always wanted them, but I always said no."

Lynne almost looked tearful. "Honey, that's sad."

"But I'm a strong-willed woman," Charity told them. "I don't know that I could allow Tom to lead, even if I tried. I'd always be trying to take control."

"I'm like that too," said Julie. "And I get spanked for it."

Lynne agreed. "Not every submissive wife gets disciplined, but many of us need it to get our marriages on track. Maybe you're like that, Charity."

Charity accepted the offer of help, but she didn't think it would work. She was just too strong a woman, and Tom just didn't have it in him to lead their marriage. She sighed as the conversation moved on to another topic.

Back in the conference hall, Tom was trying to understand. "But what if she won't submit? My wife is a wildcat."

"First you have the talk with her," said Frank. "This won't work unless you both agree that this is the best thing for your relationship."

"She might not understand right away," Joe said. "But you have to hold your ground. Refuse to allow her to have total control. Make it clear that you expect to be the boss."

"It might not be easy," said Frank. "But it might help save your marriage."

Tom looked as his hands. They were clasped together in front of him. "And if she disobeys? What if she fights me?"

"That's something you need to discuss with her," said Joe. "Lynne and I agreed that she sometimes needs to be disciplined to help her remember who is in charge of our marriage."

Frank nodded. "Many traditional marriages thrive this way."

Several of the men murmured their agreement.

"And what does the discipline involve?" asked Tom.

"It depends on your wife. You have to know what works for both of you. Most people have some combination of removal of privileges and spanking."

"I take my wife's credit card," someone put in.

"My wife gets corner time and a spanking. It helps keep her centered," said another man.

77

Tom nodded. He understood the concept, but he wasn't sure about the reality. "I don't know if I could discipline Charity," he said thoughtfully. "Not that she doesn't deserve it. She would benefit from a spanking on a regular basis."

Joe touched him on the shoulder. "Only you know what works best for your family. You should think hard, and you should consider the risks. If your marriage is already disastrous, then what do you have to lose?"

Tom let these words sink in. Frank moved onto the topic of parenting, and Tom remembered how badly he wanted children. Charity had never wanted to discuss it, and he wondered why. He decided to take the men's advice and give this a lot of thought.

Charity and Tom sat together in the big dining hall. They chatted with other couples, including Joe and Lynne. They looked at photos of other people's children, and they had a nice dinner.

Charity saw Tom watching her through most of the meal. It made her insecure about her hair and her makeup.

"What?" she asked him once.

He shook his head and smiled. "You are beautiful."

After dinner, Tom took Charity's hand. "Let's take a walk."

She looked at her watch. "I don't think we have time. We have to be at campfire soon."

"We have time," Tom insisted. He pulled Charity toward the door.

Charity couldn't remember Tom ever insisting on anything. Surprised, she followed him.

"How was your day?" he asked her. "Did you learn anything?"

She nodded, suddenly a little bit nervous in front of her husband. She wondered what he had been learning. "I think I did. I guess I never realized before just what a traditional marriage looks like. How about you?"

Tom stopped walking. He turned to her and put both her hands in his. "Charity, I love you," he said.

"I love you too, Tom," she told him with concern in her voice. He looked very serious.

"I love you," he repeated, "but I am not happy with our marriage."

Charity felt something slide through her stomach and land like a rock inside her. "You're not?"

He shook his head. "And it's my fault," he said. "I've been setting you up to take responsibility for everything. That's not fair."

She took a deep breath. "Really? You really feel that way?"

"I do, " he said. "I know we don't have long to talk right now, but let's make some changes. I want this to work."

She put her arms around his neck and hugged him close. "Me too."

The next day, the couples had a lovely breakfast. Then they gathered near the lake and listened to several people speak in turn about marriage and about all the things they had discussed the night before. When someone mentioned submission, Tom took Charity's hand.

On the way home, Charity watched Tom drive the car and wondered to herself what he was really willing to do. She knew that he and the men had talked about submission. But had they talked about discipline? Did Tom have any idea how much strength she feared it was going to take to rearrange the power exchange in this marriage?

She wanted to ask him, but she was afraid.

Instead she poked him in the side.

"Hey," said Tom. "What are you doing?"

She shook her head. She wasn't sure herself. "Nothing."

He looked at her quizzically but continued to drive the car.

She poked him again.

"Charity, cut it out," he said.

She grinned at his tone. She'd never heard him say something like that before. She put her feet up on the dashboard of the car. She wiggled her feet in the oversized sandals, and one fell of her foot.

He looked at her. "What's happening to you? You're acting like a ten-year-old."

"Nothing," she answered. "I'm just in a playful mood."

"Please put your feet down," he told her. "You're getting the dash all dirty, and you're blocking my view of the road."

She looked at her feet, and she looked at her husband. Then she bit her lower lip. "No."

He glanced at her. "Why not?"

"I just don't want to," she said.

Suddenly the heavens opened, and it dawned on Tom what was happening in his car. His wife was testing him. She was trying to figure out just what he was made of. Something in his heart and mind told her that he couldn't let her down. He pulled the car to the side of the road.

She looked momentarily panicked. "What are you doing?"

"We're going to settle this," he said. He hopped out of the driver's side and looked around. They were on a country highway with very little traffic. He went around to the passenger side and opened the door.

Charity hadn't moved her feet off the dash. She was too busy watching Tom and trying to figure out what he was going to do.

He hauled her out of the car. "If this is marriage is going to work, I'm going to have to be the boss," he told her.

She looked at him wide-eyed as he held her tightly by the forearm.

"And you're going to do what I tell you to. Understand?" he asked her.

She nodded silently.

"I think you deserve a spanking for disobedience," he said, hoping he sounded totally confident and authoritative.

She didn't laugh at him as he'd feared. Instead she nodded her head. "You're right," she said.

Encouraged he turned her around and planted twelve hard swats to the back of her shorts. She gasped.

"That really hurts!" she said, shocked.

"Good," he told her. He added twelve more.

"Tom! That hurts!" she repeated.

He smiled and gave her twelve more smacks, putting his arm into each one. "Are you ready to behave yourself?"

She nodded. Her bottom was stinging, and her heart was doing flip-flops. "Yes."

He kissed her quickly and deposited her back into the car. Then he got into the driver's side and pulled away as if nothing unusual had occurred.

They drove in silence for several minutes. Then Charity turned to Tom.

"I want to have children," she said.

Tom's face broke into a grin. "You do?"

"I want at least five," she told him.

"Five?" he asked her. "We'll have to talk about that."

She sighed and leaned her head on his shoulder. Her bottom still buzzed from the mild spanking, and her heart overflowed with love for her husband. "You're the boss," she said.

Couple Time

Becca leaned back against the fallen log and sighed happily to herself. She pulled her knees up into her chest and then turned to her husband and grinned. "I can't believe we got away for the weekend."

Dan was sitting back on his heels, poking at the fire. "Thank goodness for grandparents."

Becca laughed. She and Dan loved their four children more than anything in the world, but it was nice to have some time alone once in awhile. She crept in closer to her husband and breathed in his musky scent. Dan was an outdoorsman and always had been. He was most comfortable in a flannel shirt and jeans, sleeping out under the stars.

"How long has it been since we've camped alone?" Becca wondered out loud. She thought of their youngest daughter. "Was it before Claire was born?"

"It was before Jonah was born," Dan told her.

"That can't be right," Becca mused. At ten, Jonah was their second oldest child. "But maybe it is. Life certainly changed after Jonah."

"Two is a lot harder than one," Dan agreed. "And four is insane."

Becca put her arms around Dan's shoulders and nuzzled against his neck. "They're great kids."

"The best," Dan said. He leaned back and kissed her. Then he stood. "I can't wait to cook that fish."

Becca reached into the cooler and pulled out the trout they had caught that day. They'd cleaned them together, and Becca had even made a sauce to go with their meal. She arranged them on a pan and set them over the campfire.

Dan was searching through a grocery bag.

"What are you looking for?" Becca asked him, still watching the fish.

"I thought we brought soda," said Dan.

Becca nodded. "We did. But I think I left it in the truck. I'll go get it."

Dan shook his head. "It's too dark to be running around in the woods, hon. We'll get it tomorrow."

Becca stood and wiped her hands on her jeans. "It's not a long way to the car. I'll be back before the fish is done."

"I said no," Dan told her firmly.

Becca sat back down. She and Dan had a very traditional relationship, and he was the boss. She looked into the fire and watched it crackle. She knew he liked a soda at night, and she wished she hadn't forgotten. She looked at her husband. "It's really not far."

"Rebecca." It was a single word warning.

Becca shut her mouth.

The fish was wonderful, and the night was romantic. They cuddled together in the warmth of the fire, and Becca remembered what it was like before the children had come into her life. When they'd finished eating, Becca suddenly remembered the other thing she'd forgotten.

She'd left the chocolate in the car. For Becca, camping just wasn't camping without s'mores. She sighed.

"What's wrong?" Dan asked.

She shook her head and looked into the woods. "It's nothing. I'm going to go to the bathroom."

"You want me to go with you?" Dan asked her.

"I'll be fine," she said. The area they'd set up as a latrine wasn't far from the campsite. Dan could hear her if she called. And they'd marked the path so that they could find it easily at night.

"Be careful," Dan said.

"I will!" she called. She took a flashlight and set off toward the latrine. When she got there, she plotted her next move. She knew that the truck wasn't far away, and if she hurried she could get there without Dan knowing. Unfortunately, the bathroom was in the opposite direction as the truck. She would have to make her way in a wide arch around the campsite to avoid being caught. With her plan in place, she set off.

She made it to the truck very quickly. She grabbed the chocolate and stared for just a moment at the soda. She decided not to bring it because then Dan would know that she had disobeyed. She took the chocolate and headed back the way she came.

She walked through the woods for several minutes. She'd been camping since childhood, and she wasn't afraid of being alone in the dark. She knew how to avoid snakes, and she recognized the sounds of nature at night. But she had been overconfident in her sense of direction. It wasn't long before she realized that she had no idea where she was. She turned around to backtrack toward the truck, and she came to the conclusion that she didn't know how to do that either.

She cleared her throat and called out a few times. "Dan! Dan!"

There was no answer. Wherever she was, it was far enough away from Dan that he couldn't hear her.

She was beginning to panic as she looked to the sky for signs that she could go one way or another. She tried to remember how they had found the campsite in the first place, and what she had passed to get there. But she couldn't think, and everything looked very different in the dark. She saw a clearing ahead and thought for a moment that it might be the campsite, but as she approached she realized that it was a clearing that someone else had recently used. She sat down on a stump and thought through her options.

It wasn't long before she ripped into the chocolate.

Becca knew that she had no choice but to wait until first light. She'd been lost in the woods before, and she was fully aware that walking around in circles would only get her more confused. Propping herself up against the tree, she settled in for the night.

Dan was going to kill her.

It was still dark when Becca heard footsteps. Someone called her name. "Becca Taylor! Becca!"

She opened her eyes and shouted. "Here! I'm here!"

She jumped up and began to move. Soon she saw a young park ranger come into sight. She felt a wave of relief and then apprehension. Dan had called the park rangers in the middle of the night. He was certainly not going to be happy with her.

"I'm Becca!" she called.

The ranger looked down at her with disapproving eyes. "There are several people looking for you, young lady."

"I was lost," she offered.

"Are you hurt?"

She shook her head. "No."

"Come with me," he told her. He took a walkie-talkie out of his pocket and punched the button. "I've got her."

The ranger took Becca's arm and guided her out of the clearing and up a small hill. To her surprise, she found that they were not far from the truck at all. As they approached the dirt path where the truck was parked, she could see Dan and another man standing together. A ranger jeep was next to them. She ran toward her husband.

"Becca!" he said. He grabbed her and pulled her into his arms. "I was so worried!"

"I'm sorry," she said. "I thought I knew what I was doing."

He pushed her an arm's length away and looked at her. "What were you doing? How did you get on this side of the campsite?"

She bit her lip and tried to look sweet. "I went to the truck."

"I see." Dan's eyes were hard. He turned toward the rangers. "Thank you."

The ranger Dan had been talking to shook his hand and got back into his jeep. The ranger who had found Becca also offered his hand. "You'll be getting a bill for the search," he said.

Becca groaned. She knew it was the campground's policy to send a bill to anyone who required this kind of assistance.

"I understand," Dan said. "Thanks for your help."

The ranger looked at Becca and then back at Dan. "Sir, if I were you I would have a long talk with my wife about walking away from a campsite alone in the dark."

Dan's eyes moved to his wife. "She won't be doing this again."

"Good," said the ranger. He nodded to each of then. "Goodnight then."

They watched the rangers drive away in their jeep.

Dan turned to her. "Let's go," he said.

They walked back to their campsite hand in hand. When they returned, Becca looked up at Dan with questioning eyes. She had no doubt what was going to happen. She was just waiting for him to do it.

He looked at her for a long time. "You okay?" he asked her.

She nodded. "Yes."

"Let's sleep on this," he told her. "I'm too angry to talk about it right now."

She was both relieved and alarmed at the brief reprieve. She was glad she didn't have to face the consequences of her actions at that moment, but she was nervous to see just how angry Dan was. She climbed into the tent and changed into her sweats as Dan made sure the campfire was safely out. When he was finished, he climbed into the tent and settled in next to her. He kissed her on the forehead, and they both went to sleep.

When Becca woke up the next morning, Dan was already outside the tent. Gathering her courage, she climbed out and joined him. She perched on a little camping chair and looked him in the eye. "Good morning."

"Morning, hon," he said.

Becca was glad that he sounded so calm. "Want me to make some coffee?"

"Not yet," said Dan. "We've got something to discuss."

Her tummy flipped, and she felt herself turning into a twelve-year-old. Dan's discipline always had that effect on her.

"Stand up," he said.

She did. He pulled her sweatpants down.

"Dan!" she squealed. "Out here?" She'd known he would spank her, but she had assumed it would be in the tent.

"Oh yes," he said. "Right here."

She stood in front of him in her cotton panties with her sweatpants at her knees.

He pulled her panties down.

She felt herself blush. She knew there was no one around, but it embarrassed her to be half-naked outside in the bright morning sun. "Dan, please. Can we go into the tent?"

He shook his head. "Absolutely not. You're going to stand there like that while I make the coffee."

A whimper caught in Becca's throat. "Honey, please."

"You put me through a terrible time last night," he told her. "Now it's your turn to be uncomfortable."

She stood there, her bare bottom exposed to the cold morning air, while he went around his business. She wanted to cover herself with her hands, but she knew he wasn't going to allow it. The world was silent except for the rush of the lake and the sound of birds singing their morning songs. After several minutes he came back over to her. He had a cup of coffee in his hand.

"Kneel over the chair," he told her.

She sank down to her knees and leaned across the small camping chair. Her bare bottom was pushed out toward where the fire had been the night before.

Dan took a sip of coffee and then put it down. He put a rough hand on her bare bottom and began to rub in circles. "Did I tell you not to go to the truck last night?" he asked her.

She sucked in her breath. "Yes sir."

"And what did you do, Becca?"

Her voice came out very small. "I went to the truck."

"Is it safe to go out alone in the woods at night?" he demanded. His hand got heavier on her bottom.

"No sir," she answered, her voice quivering.

"That's right. You'd better not ever do something like this again," he told her. "You terrified me last night."

Becca began to cry. "I'm sorry, Dan. I'm so sorry."

"You should be," he told her. "You caused a lot of trouble with your disobedience."

Her tears dropped into the dirt underneath her. "I'm sorry."

"You're about to get your bottom spanked hard," he told her. "And you deserve it."

"Yes sir," she admitted.

He lifted his palm and brought it down with a smack onto her bare behind. She jolted forward and cried.

He began to spank her forcefully then, the swats falling so furiously that she couldn't distinguish one from the next. Her bottom was immediately sore and tender. Her tears came faster, and she fought to catch her breath.

"You know better than to run off like that," he scolded. "You acted like a child last night."

"I'm sorry!" she cried through her tears. She began to involuntarily swing her bottom back and forth in an attempt to escape the punishing smacks.

He swatted her harder, first on one cheek and then on another. Then he laid a volley of swats onto her lower bottom cheeks.

She shrieked. She had never been able to withstand much pain, and this spanking was the worst she had ever experienced. She could feel her bottom becoming fiery under his hand. She was sobbing openly when he stopped the spanking.

"Don't move," he told her.

She didn't hear him walk away. She couldn't hear anything through her cries. She was brought back to reality when she felt something tapping her bottom. She craned her head to see Dan standing behind her. He was holding a switch.

"Please don't," she began to murmur. "I'm sorry."

"I don't want you to even think of disobeying me again," he told her. He raised the switch, and it whistled through the air. When it made contact with her bottom, it left a thin painful line in its wake.

She yelped. It hurt so much. "I'm sorry!" she said again.

He switched her again.

She was crying and sobbing and pleading for him to stop.

He landed one more strike with the dreaded switch, and she went limp over the camp chair.

He pulled her to her feet, and her hands flew to cover her bottom. She hopped around the campsite and rubbed herself furiously while he waited for her to regain her composure.

"Pull up your sweatpants," he told her.

She obeyed him quickly, glad to know the punishment was over. Her bottom burned.

"Sit down and have some breakfast," he said, nodding toward the log where she had been sitting the night before.

She looked down at the log. "I think I'll stand," she said.

"You'll sit," he demanded.

Gingerly, she obeyed. She winced as her sore bottom made contact with the rough log. Even through her sweats it was painful.

"You stay there until I tell you to get up," he said.

They ate their breakfast together, and Dan cleaned the dishes. Becca stayed where she was, her tender bottom hurting more with each passing moment.

She looked up when she heard footsteps. Soon she saw the ranger from the night before.

"I thought I'd check on you two this morning before I head home," he said, shaking Dan's hand. "How are you?"

"Just fine," said Dan. He turned to his wife. "Becca you can get up and say hello to the ranger."

If the park ranger thought it was odd that Becca needed permission from her husband to stand, he didn't show it. He shook her hand too. "How are you doing, young lady?"

Becca looked at Dan and then back at the ranger. "I'm much better, thank you."

Becca knew that her face was stained where her tears had been. It was obvious she was upset. She had the distinct feeling that the ranger knew exactly why.

"You won't be running off again?" he asked her.

She shook her head. "No."

He smiled at her. "I'm glad to hear it."

"Would you like some breakfast?" Dan offered.

The ranger grinned. "No thanks. Just stopping by. You folks have a good day."

Becca watched the young ranger leave, and then she turned to her husband. "He seemed to know what happened here this morning."

"He suggested last night that I spank you," Dan told her.

Becca had suspected as much, but she blushed at the thought anyway.

"Back on the log," Dan told her firmly.

She looked pleadingly at him. "But my bottom hurts so much."

"It would hurt a whole lot more without your sweatpants," Dan said evenly.

It was a threat, and Becca was smart enough to take it seriously. She lowered herself back onto the log and sighed.

She watched her husband move around the campsite. She knew she was a very fortunate woman to be married to such a strong man. She renewed her commitment to be the best wife she could be.

www.ingramcontent.com/pod-product-compliance
Lightning Source LLC
Chambersburg PA
CBHW021642260626
47154CB00016BA/1791